Changing the Heart Publishing

PRESENTS

I0629663

HELP ME
Copyright 2016 by Changing the Heart Publishing

ISBN 979-8-9931887-9-9

LCCN: 2016939608

Printed in the United States

Dedication

To Aunt Sue: there is a world that exists within the world we live in. How can two walk together if they don't agree?

Moral Statement

Love yourself in spite of your self!

Table of Contents

Phase 1

Churches have whores. They go from church to church taking in everything and not caring what they get or where they get it from. They spiritual eat at their own churches and at other churches. Then, if they become sick (confused in the mind) they don't know where they got it from because they go here and there seeking what is not lost. Are you a church whore?

I must have dozed off because somehow my thoughts, spoke to me again. When I looked out of my window, I the sun was hiding behind the dark blue clouds. Taking note, I knew Mother Carol was outside on the garret rocking in her favorite porch chair. Being quietly as possible, I closed the front door. Never once did she remove her gaze to see me.

I saw how Mother Carol was staring at the two trees that were in our front yard. They both stood high

1

in the sky, but one was brown and the other one was green and brown. I sat beside her and placed my head on her lap. She put her hand on my head and stroked my hair gently.

"Can you tell the living among the dead?"

Her question threw me back, but I know that this is one of our Jesus lessons. Taking a few moments to think, I spoke, "If something is dead wouldn't it be buried under the ground, Mother Carol?"

Still not breaking her gaze, her response was, "You see those two trees?"

"Yes, I do, why?"

"They aren't under the ground. They are a part of the ground, connected to it."

"They look alike, don't they?"

"Yes, but one is brown and one is almost brown, but you already know that Mother Carol."

"People walk around on the ground alive to sin, but dead to Christ. They look like everyone else by talking and even going to service, but they are dead on the inside. Like those trees, apply them to people. They can look like they are in Christ, but sooner or later their sins will show up and they will eventually die. They look alike, but it is how they serve Jesus is what makes the difference. If you don't live for Jesus, your life is what the Word says to be like salt that is good for nothing, but to be thrown out and walked on by men."

"You are correct, Mother Carol, in your teachings, but why does Majesty Leader not teach that? Your teaching is much simpler and more understandable. I am sure all will agree."

"Over in First Timothy Chapter four, verse one it says how the Spirit will be known and how towards the end many people would be listened to things that are not of God. Believe that the teaching is made by demons. Gracie, demons inspire all false teachings. False teachings binds, only the truth sets free. Basically, my daughter, he cannot teach what he does not know or have."

I know that I am not to question my parents, but Mother Carol allowed me to question her about the scriptures that she teaches me. However, I would use this opportunity to ask her other questions, "How important is it to understand what we don't see?"

"Gracie, God is a spirit, and we cannot see HIM, but by faith we know that HE created everything. Before you can explain what, you see, you must first understand what you do not see."

"Why are we here if others do not believe as we do? The two are not to mix, right?"

"In time we will leave, but I pray it is not too late."

"Mother Carol, I thank Jesus every night for giving you unto me. I have learned more from you than I do in all the services I have sat in. What do you mean by you pray it's not too late?"

She did not respond to my question, but she did say, "Gracie there is a spiritual world here you cannot see and there is the natural world you do see. You can't see love, good, bad, and evil because they are spiritual. It is when they are in a natural form that you can see them. You my daughter must be strong and listen carefully."

I scooted closer since she doesn't talk loud when she talked about the spirits. I was always eager to hear what she says. When I stop making noise, Mother Carol stated, "You have a name and so do evil spirits."

"How do they have names?"

"Don't you have a name?"

"Yes."

"If I walked up to you and Father James and said you come here. Which one of you would move?"

"Neither because you didn't call our name."

"If I said Gracie come here, will Father James move?"

"No. That is not his name."

"Same with spirits. You must call them by name. It is the only way they will answer you."

"How do you know their name?"

"You must rely on God the Spirit to fill in what you lack."

"Oh."

She must have felt that I did not truly get what she was saying. Mother Carol spoke, "I will only name a few, but listen. If someone has the spirit of mental illness, which we call crazy, it has other spirits connecting to it like: insanity, madness, and hallucinations. If someone has the spirit of cursing, it has in its tow the spirit of Blasphemy, gossip, backbiting, and belittling. If someone has the spirit of sexual impurity, then lust, fantasy, masturbation, homosexuality, adultery, fornication, and incest."

She did not look at me when she said, "Gracie you must learn all you can by me and study this King James verse bible as if your life depends on it for it will. You, my child, are a deliverer and you must be familiar with the spirits that link up."

"Link up?"

"Just like a chain it has many hooks, demons are like that. The first link is the name, and the rest are hooked to it. It is one chain with many loops correct?"

7

"You mean demons have one name, but many other links to hold the chain together?"

"Yes, and always keep in mind that fear is false evidence appearing real."

"I will, but what is a deliverer?"

"Someone that sets the captive free, Gracie."

"How am I to do that?"

"With Jesus."

"With Jesus?" I repeated back to her.

"Yes, Gracie, you can't do anything without Jesus."

I gave my mother a light kiss and prayed before turning in for the night. Once asleep I stood in front of a shabby, but worn closed door. It was brown with a deep, dark color of blood oozing all around the white ceiling to the cool wooden floor. For some reason, I was not afraid. I walked closer to the door and heard if I

8

open a door no man could close it unless I say so. Feeling confident of the rephrased scripture, I reached up and touched the knob. I jerked my hand back and let go of it as I screamed inside my mouth because the doorknob was scotching hot.

Glancing down at my white palm, it turned pink with blisters. I wanted to get angry, but feeling the throbbing of my hand wouldn't let me. That time I took the helm of my dress and quickly turned the knob. When the door swung open it made an enormous echo sound as it hit the wall. There before me was the darkest night I had ever seen. The entry to me was like midnight. I walked closer to the door and with no warning I staggered backwards. I began to gasp and vomit because disgusting odor of blood, spoiled meat, and strong urine pierced my nostrils and entered my mouth.

Taking a deep breath inside my clothing, I stepped my foot into this unknown territory and from the first step, the room begun to spin out of control. When I brought my second foot in, I looked down and saw under my feet were dry brittle bones, human bones none the less. Instantly the prophet Ezekiel came to mind and how he was in the valley of dry bones. Gulping hard and having the feeling of being sick, I wanted to run, but when I turned to do that, the door slammed shut by making a loud enormous noise. Turning back around I knew I had to continue on or stand there and wait for the unknown. Each step I took, the bones began to snap and crack as if they were sticks.

I dared not look down again for if I did, I might lay alongside them. At that moment, sounds of people wailed in pain reached my ears. Their cries were more like agony. Tears strolled down my small face for them; however, I kept walking. Although, the more I walked the darker my journey became. I felt alone and scared.

With each intended step, shadows were reaching out for me and grabbing at me. I would yank away from them. I wanted to scream, but Mother Carol said screaming was a sign for lack of faith; therefore, I did not open my mouth to give into fear. I continued walking and repeating loudly for all to hear, "The Lord is with me. I will not be afraid. Jesus will not ever leave me alone!"

Suddenly, I heard a soft childlike voice taunting me as pale black arms and hands reached out at me. "We're coming for you. We're coming for you. We're coming for you. We're coming for you."

I woke up, screaming and Mother Carol came into my small-lit room and blurted out in a tearful tone, "What's wrong my child? My daughter what's wrong?"

She saw that I was trembling and I didn't speak as I sat upright on my bed. Leaving the door ajar, she rushed over to me in speed. Mother Carol draped her arms around me. Whispering softly in my ear as not to be heard, "Shush daughter, you and I serve a God above all God's and all our lives we have served HIM, but HE has a name and it is Jesus. HE will deliver you."

I didn't say a word as Mother Carol persistently held me as I cried like the child I was. I could only sniffle and weep in her bosom as the dreams taunt me more and more. Soon as my cries stop she placed the cover back on me and left out the room. I turned my head and saw she left the door ajar. I felt somewhat at peace. Every other night since my eighth birthday fast approach, I dreamt of hell and death. I didn't understand it, but I knew my parents did and they don't have to tell me anything. For it is the way of our church.

Once Mother Carol said, her life changed the day she came here when she was fourteen. I remembered her saying that she was a chosen vessel and was due to bring forth a chosen vessel on the eleventh time. Every year since then, she bore me a brother, until I was born.

Speaking of my brothers, I missed them, but I was not allowed to see them because they trained on the other side of the camp, preparing for the invaders when they came. Half of me wish to be a boy because as girls we had to prepare our bodies in case we are picked as the Majesty Leader girl, whatever that means. I knew that I was the miracle my mother waited on.

On that night, I could not sleep again. The nightmare was too real and disturbing to enter rest again. I got up and peep from a distance. I watched Mother Carol as she sat with the fire to her right. The house was clean, and the outside night was quiet. The only sounds were flames that crackled in the open fireplace, as she slowly and gently, she rocked back and forth.

Every so often she would take a deep sigh then she would stop and start again. The way her long sleeved matched her dark blue, long skirt, and white apron attached made her look of purity and wholesome. From that point I wanted to talk to her, but I noticed she was withdrawn and sad. Father James was gone into prayer with the other watchmen of the church and his return would soon be to come. Ceasing the opportunity,

I walked easily toward her and the floor gave way that I was coming. She stopped rocking and looked up at me.

With her warm smile and relaxed look she glanced up and opened her arms for me to come near. Speeding up my steps to her, the embrace was inviting, but somehow it touched me. I saw that I was going to great efforts to make her smile by playing with her loose curl while I sat in her lap. She held me and patted me on my head like she usually did. The smell of her clothing reaped of lemons and mint, my favorite.

She stared down at me with gloom and still she managed to say slowly, "Tonight is the night Majesty Leader names the chosen child for the New Era."

"Who do you think will be picked or do you think I will be picked?"

Mother Carol took in a deep breath as she responded, "My child, there are many others and you might be chosen, but I hope another child is named the successor for this New Era. For there is a grave responsibility, that will be placed on the young lady and she must complete the task."

"Will you still love me if I am not picked?"

She stopped rocking and looked at me with a solemn face. I gave her an inviting look. Mother Carol declared with joy, "Gracie, I will love you from our Heavenly Father Jesus and back a million times fold. Remember you are loved no matter what the outcome is. Just know that God knows all things and HE knows what is best for us no matter what we think."

She took off the locket she always kept on her neck. She placed about my neck and kissed my cheek. In my mind I vowed not to ever lose it. I gave my mother a hug and noticed she smiled. Seconds later Father James opened the door and interrupted our moment. Mother Carol spoke softly as she kissed me good night, "Get down and hurry along to back bed. Your father is here."

"Yes, Mother."

Giving her a night kiss, I got down and hurried along towards my room. I did not touch Father James because he just came out of prayer with the Majesty Leader and he is not to be talked to by the children. By passing him I went towards my room. Instead of going to bed, I did not. I did walk in my room but stood by the cracked door to listen. I could see Father James as he stood in front of Mother Carol while she rocked. She looked up at him and began to cry. He stooped beside her to comfort her but that did not help. Mother Carol stop rocking and spoke, "My husband this has to stop! Gracie can't continue to endure these dreams before he choose. She is only a child! James she is our child!"

In his stern tone, I heard him tell Mother Carol, "And so was Jeremiah."

I crawled onto the floor. Luckily the wall counter covered me. In earshot, I could hear well as my parents. For some reason, she stopped rocking. She look up at him and in a plea shook her head no. My mother was in tears as her crackled voice pleaded, "No, James not my Gracie. Please not my baby, Gracie. She is our only daughter. Why won't he choose another girl? Minister Warren has five girls why not one of theirs?"

Having a surprised look of joy, I spoke in my head as my hand touched my chest "He picked me? Majesty Leader picked me."

Father James with his assured tone replied, "If we love her we will start giving her the drink. I know you don't approve and you wish we would have left,

18

but there is nowhere else for us to go. We have nothing and you have nowhere to go. You know we can't depend on the world and their way of living in order for us to survive. We don't know of any other way."

I knew this was important because my parents have never disagreed. My Mother spoke with power when she stated, "My husband you don't know what this entire means? You think you know but I promise you, you really don't have an idea, mislead you are. You need to start professing Jesus as your Lord and Savior. I can't stop what is to come, but in this flesh, I too am ordained to a calling that I can't escape, but spiritually I know I have to teach Gracie what can help her."

Father James almost shouted at her when he replied, "You have always said that to me. Even your parents in the community thought you were always drunk with some kind of wine, for you talked like no other."

Using a quieter tone, she stated, "Husband James, there is much more to me than you know. I have always felt that this life is not right. I don't know exactly why? But you know I strongly believe what I am speaking because of my Christian upbringing."

"Silence! This silly talking you are doing. You have talked this way for many years, and I have not reported of your foolishness because I don't want to be look upon as having a mad wife. But, if you continue to speak of such, I will be forced to tell Majesty Leader and the Elders that you maybe an intruder."

My mother continued to cry as she spoke softly. She sat up in the rocker to say, "What if I take Gracie and ran away? She couldn't do it. *What if I take her now and no one will know where we are? We can leave right now*. Maybe I could get help before it is too late. That way no one could find us and she would be safe to be normal. I knew two people that would be glad to help Gracie."

No one spoke for what seemed like hours. Father James finally said with stern words, "You want your sons shun from the community? They will be damned and not have eternal passage because of their linage to you. You want all their hard work and ethics to be of none avail?"

"I don't want that for them at all. They are boys and it took us many years before we were blessed with Gracie. I want her away from this type of life. If I can't help her, I hope she finds the strength to do it when the time comes. The Word tells me that if I ask Jesus to guide me HE will. All I have to do is ask HIM."

For the first time in my life, I heard my father be meaningfully and indulgent as he said, "The Word also tells us to beware of false prophets and if you take her then, my wife Carol, I must kill you."

She slumped back into her rocker and sobbed silently. Father James got up as he kneeled to her side to comfort her, "There is no other way for us to get to Heaven. If we go any other way to heaven and not go through God, we are no better than liars and thieves because we disobey. I don't know about you, but I can't do it. I can't get before my God and have him turn me away because I didn't listen."

"My husband James, I just can't do it, either. They already have our sons. She is the youngest of our eleven and our only girl. There are other girls just as fair as ours."

22

"Majesty Leader can see who the one is, he needs. He has been in prayer for weeks to choose the right one and it has been our Gracie. We should be honored to have her chosen by God to allow our child to partake in such a dedicated ceremony."

"My husband James, you don't think it is wrong that we cannot call on the name of Jesus during our services? We must continue to refer to our God as God and not by his name Jesus that is revealed to us in the New Testament, in the King James Version?"

Father James did not reply. Mother Carol went on to say, I am forever grateful but to grasp at it all, I cannot. Gracie is an original. She has a calling upon her that must be fulfilled. She has a mighty work to do for Jesus, and she is."

Father James cut her off to say, "Just like you, a so-called preacher's woman, to rebuke Satan with the

Word of God and to deliver peoples souls out of Hell or is she is an optimistic, a dreamer, and tries to find the truth in everything? Yes, my wife, Carol, she is you, but smaller."

"So, you think I am wrong, don't you? My husband James, many years ago before here, you were taught that Jesus is real, and the full Word of God is real. Don't you remember when we met? You were baptized in the name of Jesus."

"Shush, woman! I remember, but you must apply Majesty Leader's bible and leave the King James Version bible alone. I should have burned it a long time ago."

"Demons inspire people to do things that are unlike Jesus by corrupting the Word of God. Majesty Leader mentions things that fit his cause and not the right cause. I have sons that I haven't seen in years. I grieve on the inside and to think the spirit of disobedience operates in you as well as in I, but I have tried to right my wrongs before it is too late!"

As to influence my mother Father James said, "As for you being in error, I do believe you have that spirit operating in you. It is not about if you are wrong, it's what's more important? What you want or what Majesty Leader says God wants from his faithful servants, as we ourselves are?"

"Of course, you know that it is what Jesus wants, but I don't think this is it. I can't imagine this is it. I thought it would have been me to stop it, but it wasn't. It's in me! Evil is being more revealed as time goes and I'm a hostage like she will be. It doesn't matter how much this ministry tries to help because if we don't get Jesus right nothing we do will ever matter."

"It is not for you to imagine it is not even what you want. It is settled. We will do it before the invaders come in to attack us. Majesty Leader says we only have a little over three years before they try to come in. Our sons along with other sons are being trained as we speak in the army that is to protect you women and daughters. I will be there with our sons as we glorify God in Heaven. I won't live to see The Prophesy, and neither will they, but at least we would see it when we look down from HIS throne and know we did our part."

"Majesty Leader does not mention Hell. He only tells one side of things. He tells us how good and merciful God is, but he doesn't say how Hebrews Chapter ten, verse thirty-one say how bad things could get if we disobey our living God. He does not even mention that anything that will really help our souls and you know I am right." Father James kept quiet to think.

Mother Carol tried to persuade him by saying, "What does the scripture say about false teaching, since you mentioned it?"

"It talks about being servants of things that are wrong. It says how you speak as you believe and if you believe in HIM you will be holy and in a Godly state."

"You brought me here under false pretenses and this religion took me in. You know in your heart that the King James Version bible is correct, and Jesus Christ is the only true way to live. You recited the verse perfectly because you know them as the Word of God and not what Majesty Leader has spoken of. If my parents had accepted our love, we would not be in this predicament."

"That was a long time ago and that life we once knew was dead to us and dead to me."

"My husband James, you know this church is in Doctorial Error that is facing Blasphemy on the highest level. This is more of a Religious cult than a church trying to live right for our Heavenly Father."

Mother Carol became quiet as her tears dried. Father James did not say a word. They stayed in this position for a very long time. Each was engrossed in thought as I was afraid to move. Luckily Father James said, "My wife Carol, you must stop this foolish talking and do what you must. You sound like those crazy people that Majesty Leader speaks of. No wife of mine will be as such. I command you this, starting tomorrow you must tell her, and she must start the drink."

"Tomorrow!"

"Yes, time is at hand, and our Heavenly Father is to return soon."

Reaching inside his long coat, he pulled out a formula. He handed it to Mother Carol and just held it clinched in her palms.

"Take it and do it correctly because if it fails, we all fail. We all will go to Hell for eternity."

"What about the other little girls that has gone before Gracie? They all had girls and were banished from the community. Their parents aren't even allowed to see them or their grandchildren. This could happen to our Gracie, and I don't think I can bare the fact of not seeing my daughter."

"That is them. He says the false children have to come first before the real ones, like with Abraham and Haggai. Ishmael came first, then Isaac. Now, is time for the boy and it is through Gracie, the chosen vessel."

"It is no secret that I have doubts my husband, James. Don't you think he could be wrong and mess up her life? Without repentance there is no remission of sins."

"Just like picking apples. There is a chance that we can get snake bitten and there is a chance we may not. Majesty Leader has spoken and that is all we need to know."

Very softly and very quietly, Mother Carol spoke to Father James as if she was tired and weary, "My husband, demons influence people to become carried away with strange doctrines. They then will believe in another Jesus that is not the Jesus of the King James Bible. These people will ignore what God says and fall by the wayside. According to Hebrew Chapter three, Verses nine through fifteen talk about how we can get in error and how our forefathers disobeyed God and they were in the wilderness for forty years. Because they disobeyed God, they were denied the promise. It also says while it is today, right now to lift up your fellow workers in Christ. But, if we hold on and not doubt when we hear HIS voice there is no way we can be found with unbelief."

Father James only continued to stare at Mother Carol. She sighed, and said with disbelief, "You have not understood anything I have said and for that you and our sons will lose your lives in heaven and find it in Hell."

"I am beginning to believe you are still overtaken as an Englishwoman with this Jesus Christianity and not of one in the true faith as you have heard for years now through our many Majesty Leaders."

Mother Carol did not say another word to him. I did not understand how Father James could not see what was going on. I remembered that he can't see unless Christ allows him to see and he can't show him unless, he wants to see it. Until then, my father will remain blind and on the outside of Christ. I eased into my room and lain down. The moon was shining ever so brightly through my uncovered window. Everything was so bright outside and so peaceful, but somehow, I didn't feel the peace.

Easing down under the covers I prayed. Soon as I finished praying and pulled the covers up to my neck I turned over as Mother Carol came in. She sat on my bed with her back to the door and her face in the moon. My back was to her, but I can hear her sobbing silently. In a tone she spoke with an apology, "Gracie I never meant for you to be a part of this. I desire so much to take you away, but I am forbidden. I wish we were different, but this is a part of our destiny. Please forgive me, daughter."

I turned over and we stared into each other's face. "He chose me, didn't he?"

Shaking her head solemnly yes, Mother Carol placed her hands over her mouth and responded, "Yes daughter, he chose you because there was never anyone else to choose from. Telling the people he had to choose one was a ploy because you were born just for this purpose."

Seeing the pain upon her it grieved me, and I was but a child. I knew I had to grow up and help comfort her for allowing the Majesty Leader to include me in his plans.

"Mother, in good conscious we are doing what we have been taught. If I am chosen, then it is my destiny to fulfill whatever it is. If it starts with me, it must end with me. I know you love me, but I have to do it. Your Jesus will protect me just like you said HE would."

One can only assume that she handled what I said with cheer because she reached down and squeezed me so hard. I almost lost my breath. Gradually she lessened the hug and spoke, "I am going to be by your side every step of the way. It is not going to be as you think but I am here for you and I love you, my Gracie."

"Mother Carol, I love you, too, good night."

That night I knew that my life would not be the same. I knew I must grow up and help lead the people, but I didn't know how. Mother Carol was happy again and to see her smile made me smile. I slept like a princess and was glad I had my mother's joy back. The next morning, I washed up and said my morning prayers. When I walked out my room, my breakfast was ready.

"Gracie, you are off house duties for the next year. You are forbidden to play with the others for the threat of contamination, and you are not allowed to pass the porch for it is unholy. You are to remain here at all times until Majesty Leader sends for you within a month and a half. It will be your eighth birthday. You will have a party then with all the candy you want."

Candy, I thought. This type of food was of the world, and we could never indulge unless the Majesty Leader sermon for you.

"Mother Carol, I thank you for your commands."

I didn't question because if I did that meant that I was not being submissive to my parents. It meant I was rebelling and wild. We didn't ask questions, and we did what we were told. I assumed it was because Majesty Leader has something in store for me.

Breaking my thoughts, Mother Carol handed me something to drink. I knew it was from Father James.

With perfection, I swallowed the drink. It was bitter but sweet. It didn't taste half bad. This went on for days. Every day during meals, I was to drink the drink and at night, Mother Carol would check on me and to make sure I was okay. One night she came to see me, I was crying. She came in and asked, "Are you okay?"

Between my many tears I removed the white covers back and revealed that blood was everywhere. I looked up, and spoke, "I am bleeding, and I don't know why. I have not disobeyed, and I have not done anything that is not right in the sight of God."

"My Gracie, oh my Gracie, it has begun."

She explained to me what was happening to my body and how all girl children endure the same thing

36

every month just like she said. Six weeks past and Mother Carol came into my room early that evening, and said, "You know it's your birthday."

"I do."

She sat on the bed. I stared at my mother for she was not herself. She indicated, "Gracie, promise me that whenever you are afraid that you will call on the name of Jesus. There is no power in the name of God. All power is in the name of Jesus. You must do this is you expect our Lord to save you, even if I your mother come at you, please call on the name of Jesus."

"Mother, I will."

"Don't forget what I have taught you and remember not to mention it to anyone living here."

"Mother Carol, I will not forget, and I know that others here do not believe as we do."

"Good girl. Come along, Majesty Leader sermons you."

This is the event that they have been preparing me for. Mother Carol dressed me in pretty pink hair bows. I had no idea where they came from because we were permitted to wear anything to attract attention. She even placed perfume all over me and showed me a mirror. I was adorable. Before Father James came to me, Mother Carol spoke, "It will hurt but remember it is for the New Era. Take yourself to a happy place and it will only last a few minutes."

"Okay. I am happy to do it for the people."

When my Father James took me before the Majesty Leader he opened the door for me. He is about my oldest brother age and very handsome. The curly locks on his head were of brown and black. The way they bounced would catch your attention and you would watch them. His eyes were the blackest I had ever seen and his smile was whiter than any I knew of. His skin color was like no other for it was smooth as well as smells good. He is not what I expected. However, it was something in the way he smiles.

Normally he is covered up at services and no one sees him but the Elders. Today he is allowing little ole me to see him in his natural state of being himself. I knew he sounded young but to see if for myself was unusual. Mr. Warren did a short ceremony for Majesty Leader and me. He said we were now ready to do whatever in front of God. To me, this means I must be married because I felt that he and I were connected. After the moment was over, he left us alone. I continued to stand unsure of what to do, but Majesty Leader came closer and guided me to a small table in his room.

There he fed me all the candy and cookies I could devour. I had only heard of such things as ice cream, sweet color water, chips, and doughnuts, but there I was, eating all the things a girl gets on her eighth birthday. I had so much fun with Majesty Leader. He and I played games as we drank the red color water he called wine. He made me laugh. We even danced and I had so much fun even though, I got dizzy from time to time. He told me he like my hair and my pretty dress because I was beautiful. He even said, he liked me a lot and I smell good.

At first, I was afraid, but as the night went along, I couldn't help but to like him. He makes me smile when I feel down. To ease my mind, we played hand games, and we wrestled. I thought the experience would be bad, but it was really nice. He even told me that I was young, beautiful, and he loved me. That made me happy. He was kind and proclaimed that he wanted me for I was the fairest of them all. Before long we were playing in our underwear. I didn't like it, but when he showed me a mirror and spoke how I didn't look eight, I took it all in. My breast was bigger than the Minister Warren's oldest daughter and she was twelve.

My hips were thicker, and my behind was very round, which, he added. He said it was normal for us to be like this because we went before God, and I believe him. If it weren't true, Mother Carol would not allow it. Majesty Leader would hold me in his arms, and he would make me feel calm. He was very kind and affectionate to me. His smile would give me a peace that says I am with you and only you.

Whenever he would touch me with his hands, I liked it. I couldn't wait for him to touch me and smile the way he does. He was kind, funny, and charming. He told me that if things went well that I would be the last of the fairest that he would know of. That pleased me for I have heard that many went before me, but he was confident in our meetings that I would be the only one for him.

The more we talked the more he had me to drink. I drank so much wine that I didn't remember falling out on the bed. I recall Majesty Leader staring into my face. At that age, I just needed to be near him. I could not understand it, but my sense of being with him was too stout to ignore. I smiled at him before closing my eyes. With his head full of brown locks, he leaned into me and gave me my first kiss before speaking huskily, "Keep your eyes upon me. Watch my curls if you must, but don't tense up. This may sting and I promise you it will be good, and it will not last long."

My eyes did not open fast enough. I felt a sharp pain below my stomach. I began staring at Majesty Leader's curls as he directed. He said, "Gracie, I am here for you and this is a natural affection that young girls have with the man she goes before God."

I became calm as the pain simmered. He waited a few more moments then he began moving inside of me deeper. His face gave me comfort as I stared at him. My legs trembled as he held them high in the air. Completely, I was lost. I only heard of a man hurting a woman, but I was not a woman I was a child. The tears began to shower my face as he said with each thrust, "We are doing this for God, Gracie. Think what you are going to accomplish when this is over with? You are blessed and God has shown favor on you, be thankful."

It didn't feel like I was doing this for God. I was in pain and my leader was the one giving me this pain.

Majesty Leader stopped talking and started grunting and going fast for what seemed like years until he fell limp. I didn't know what to do as he got off of me. He pulled me close to lay beside me. I saw myself laying there helpless. Soon as he was sound asleep, I got up and saw blood everywhere. The tears flowed all the more.

Majesty Leader awoke and saw my discomfort. He put a sheet under me as his persuading voice consoled me. "You have to lie back down. I will not hurt you any more tonight. It will get easier and my Gracie you were wonderful. You are no longer a child, but a woman."

I didn't feel like a woman as Majesty Leader fell asleep, with his arms tightly about me. I on the other hand could not sleep. I saw myself praying for forgiveness and for someone to help me. I did not want this man nor did I want him making me ache again. But, unfortunately that did not happen. I was not allowed to leave the room. I had all my meals there and I was not prohibited to see anyone.

Every night, sometimes three times a day, Majesty Leader came into me and we did the same thing. I took it that he could not get enough of me because he kept going between my legs. To put me at comfort, he would play games with me and make me laugh. Once the laughing stopped the routine began by him making me drink wine. When I would feel dizzy I would lay down. It did not take me long to know that the wine made the pain more tolerable.

Once I was on the bed, he would get on top of me and all I could do was lay there. If I did not tighten my body the pain did not hurt at all, but once I would frown or show displeasure, the pain would last long,

45

and he would be on top of me longer. So, I would lay there and allow him to have his way with my young body. Strange enough, I was beginning to like it. Before I knew it, he would hold me as he slept.

Like always I would lay there in semi pain, semi joy, and some panic because it did not feel right, but I have guidelines to obey and if I didn't who knew what would happen. The happiest part was I was enjoyed the drinking and the way he made me feel when he would enter me. It no longer felt wrong because God knows and Mother Carol knows. I am not doing anything wrong in fact I am going to help the entire church family go to heaven.

The more he entered me the more I wanted him to. My body would be on pins for him, and I didn't get it. There were many things not explained to me. Male and female interactions were not one. As the days dragged, my horror and my thoughts of was it right or wrong were gone. If it wasn't right, but it felt right. After the first few times, I practicality welcomed it. That experience was mind bottling and the more we did it the more it became a part of me.

On the other hand, Mother Carol didn't tell me about the pain of a man sleeping with someone they love. She didn't even tell me what all would occur during my time with him. But, she did tell me that she would be there for me and that meant more to me. He was right, it did get easier to drink and lay still. I enjoyed the way he was happy when he entered me. My body took a life of its own. I learned how to meet his mighty thrust and how he liked my legs. Majesty Leader made me feel like a woman. He said I was, but I was a child.

He would take his time to enter me and the sounds he made when he was on top of me were like angels singing. When I felt down, I would quickly remember that it was not about me. It was about everyone there, depending on me to make him happy. When I would be alone, I would think of ways he would like to be happy when he was in me and no more sadness occurred. It gave me gladness to let him take me the way he did and every night when he finished, he would hold me close to his heart.

I even heard him tell me that I was the best in the entire compound and no one was better. To hear him say I was the best gave me delight. I began to loosen up and allow my legs to fall easily when he crawls between them. After seven more days of drinking and letting him get on top of me would come to a close. I became sad. I did not want to leave him,

48

and I did not want him to have another, but there was nothing I could do. I had prayed that our time together worked out because he did not need to have another one take my place. That would be devastating and hurtful.

On our last night he said he wanted to try something different, and he hoped I would like it. Majesty Leader also said it would take all night to finish it, but we must do it for we are in our final hours and everything depended upon him and me getting it right. The first thing he had me do was get on all fours on the edge of the bed. I was nervous and he could tell that I was scared. But, that was quickly missed as he reminded me of the greater good that I did. He got behind me and entered me in the same hole he usually enters.

It was odd, but different in deed. He would push against me harder, and I would fall to my knees and he would encourage me to get up and try to hold my weight in one place. That worked until he got carried away and had me to put my head in the bed and until he finished what he started. Quickly, like always I had to lie down and wait as he always ordered me to do. Hours later, he climbs on top of me and did it all over again.

The aching was bearable because of the look of peace on his face that gave me happiness. I also reminded myself that it was for heaven and everyone. When he finished in our final hours, he lay beside me, and said, "I do believe that you are the last one for me. You were perfect and don't think down because you have helped me out in more ways than you can know."

"Majesty Leader, I won't ever forget you."

He used his hands to brush my hair. For the first time, I felt like I really did a good deed. The next morning, I was given grave instructions regarding my spirit before I was allowed to go back home. A part of me did not want to leave. I wanted to stay with him. Strange enough, I wanted to see him. I needed to see him before I left, but I was prohibited. They denied me the last thing I wanted and there was nothing I could do. Grief struck me and I questioned myself, if I would be in his arms and bed again.

When I did return, Mother Carol was crying hysterically. I wanted to cry, too, but had to have a happy persona so the light could shine within me. No one was allowed to touch me, not even my own mother. The Orders spoke that it may do damage to my soul and to the work Majesty Leader tried to perfect in me. She could only look at me and weep. I didn't think she knew just how I was dying on the inside to be near our leader. I don't think anyone cared about my feelings.

Father James was gone back into prayer with the other Elders. They all have to be on one accord in order for the meeting to work. I hope it did work because I did not want to drink wine or let him enter my body again without proper permission. It was different and it has changed my life. Being that I was touched be Majesty Leader, none of the young would be suitors were allowed to come after me. It was heartbroken, but that was that.

When it came time for the blood to come, it did not. I complained that I didn't feel good and later the church doctor Naomi told my parents the meeting between Majesty Leader and I worked. They told me that I would get bigger because for the New Era coming and that was a good thing. Everyone in our church was happy and I thought I would have seen Majesty Leader, but I did not. They brought me all kinds of things and still no one could touch me, but the church doctor

Naomi. It bothered me some for I desperately needed to

feel my mother holding me as she did that night I found

out I was the one.

Whenever I discussed Jesus, my stomach would

ache horribly. I learned that demons try early to attack

children. Mother Carol spoke since I was who I was,

and demons were after me. She clearly told me that the

majority of demons seem to enter during childhood.

She said that it was important to provide children with

proper spiritual covering and parents who are involved

in sin open the door for demons to attack the children.

Mother Carol said that what a father does affect

the children the most because he was the head and he

had the most authority. I learned that demons could

enter children in the womb through curses. If parents

don't want the child this gives demons legal rights to

the child. However, I was surprised when I heard that children who have been sinned against usually have many problems in adulthood.

Mother Carol went on to say how demons start very early in life and attempt to build upon a foundation through active sin as the child grows into adulthood. Salvation at an early age will destroy much of the enemy plans for the child's life and that was why she taught me Jesus in order to save me. She told me in my case the devil is trying to bring on this as a bad experience and cause abnormal grief to destroy me. But, one thing the enemy had not counting on was her being of God. He had no idea that she would teach me all she could in the short time and how as long as she had breath, I would be given on to Jesus for HIS use and HIS power.

Nevertheless, she became more adamant as the lessons were intense and consecutive. Mother Carol started testing me harder and harder. She would say KJV and a scripture. I had to know where the scripture was she would be talking about. I even had to understand the time frame of how men and women dressed. The culture back then was not that much different but yet I had to know it in order to fully explain the Gospel.

Sometimes it got confusing trying to listen to Majesty Leader on service days because I knew he was contradicting the true Word of God. The good thing was, after his services, Mother Carol and I would go back home, and she would show me the right word in our bible. I enjoyed that. One day she decided it was time for me to be born of the water baptism before it was too late. She put on my cotton gown for me and filled the tub up with water. She explained to me the symbolic meaning as I sat in the tub. Mother Carol had me to repeat. "Jesus I have sinned, and I fallen short. I ask you to save my soul as you forgive me of my sins. I believe you died for me on the cross and I know there is nothing else but the cross for me. Amen."

I repeated it and the next thing I knew she dunked me under the cool water. When she lifted me up, it felt strange, but new. I knew that going down in the water did not save me, but somehow I had the sensation of what it meant to really be born again. I got out and dried off. Next, she explained to me the symbolic meaning of communion and all the what if's if I am not really ready before I was allowed to partake in it.

I knew I was ready and had no fear about what tomorrow may bring. I also do not fret the shortcomings because I was saved. Jesus gave up the ghost on the cross for my sins. To live for Christ was more than just confessing that Jesus was my Lord and Savior. I have a personal relationship with him because I spoke in tongue as soon as I finished the communion. It is the best feeling ever and since that day, I was different. I saw things differently than ever. She told me that I would need it in the upcoming events.

Although, I was saved and born again, it did not stop the sounds of children taunting me in my ears every night. They would laugh at me and when I awaked, I would be alone. Sometimes, I would visually see a child, lurking at me. But, when I would get up they would disappear. It boggled my mind and vexed me because those visions took life form.

Mother Carol explained that demon spirits tried to attack my sanity to make me appear foolish and for me to doubt the very existence of Christ. She told me that I must be strong for if the spirits were appearing in the day then I am truly on the right path. I must admit that it did get hard because everything I tried to understand made me doubt. However, when that spirit of doubt came, I rebuked it and went on.

Sometimes, no matter how I try to ignore the taunting, I could still hear it. I thought back to the teachings I was receiving and how those words had strengthen me. I also remember Mother Carol saying that Gadara means walled and how the enemy was well organized; therefore, we must be also when it came to the things of Jesus. Mother Carol clearly explained that curses gave demons the legal right to enter the bloodline and carry out their wicked plans.

She told me since I obtained the Holy Spirit that I must listen. She pointed out to me in the Word how you have to have Jesus's Spirit in you. We *must worship Jesus in Spirit and in truth, but how can we if we don't have HIS spirit*? Is the question, I would often ask, and Mother Carol told me I have the Spirit others don't. She stated that I understood scriptures and knows when the Spirit speaks, but to unveil the Word is called Revelation knowledge.

This morning when I woke up, I did not feel right. I didn't like being chosen but above all Mother Carol and Naomi made my imprisonment fun and they never once told me that I had a child inside of me. I kind of knew because I was getting a little bigger and felt something moving. Naomi prepared to leave because it was about to storm, so she went to gather her things. Mother Carol waited until the doctor was in the room, she lip to me, "Drink this and keep your mouth shut about it. It will help you and maybe save you."

I didn't question her. I drank the tan tasting liquid. Naomi came out the room and left the house. Moments later I began to hurt none-stop. It is not time for the New Era, but it made me ache. Like never before, I balled over and clinched my stomach from the discomfort. Mother Carol rushed to the door and called out for Church doctor Naomi quickly. Rain began to fall, but in speed, she rushed back, and placed me on the bed. I had the feeling that of constipation, but it was not from my butt. She opened my legs and had me to push like I was going to the bathroom. I did and nothing happened.

I could feel her touching me and doing something to me. The more she told me to push the more the baby would not move. She peeped up at me with trembling and terror as she yelled out, "It's stuck!"

Mother Carol did not move as I kept on crying. Somehow my cries were among the thundering and my tears not heard for the harsh rain. My mother sat there with her face to the window as if she was praying. As Naomi continued working with me off and on, I had to push and hold it, over and over. I did as she commanded with tears and sweat. The more I cried out the more the lightning brightened the room. I felt like I was ripping from every angle below from pain I would not ever forget.

For hours, if not days the pain would come and go. They never explained to me that part. In fact, I had been almost clueless about everything.

"Push again with all your strength!" She yelled out. I closed my eyes and pushed with everything I had. When I felt the release of my body, lightening hit something as a very loud noise was heard on this stormy night. Naomi yelled out as she fell over dead, "What kind of baby is this!"

I discarded what she spoke for I was relieved the pain was over. I had never felt so tired in my entire life. My eyes searched for my mother as she graciously paced her steps and took the child out of Church doctor Naomi arms. I could see my child. It was a big bloody child and did not cry. Mother Carol held the child in her arms bloody and all as she never once glanced at me.

Her eyes were fixed on the child in her arms. I raised my head up higher to see what went on. Lightning struck across the sky, and I saw a dark figure holding the baby. It didn't look like my mother, but I knew it had to be her. She lifted the baby up and tilted her head to the sky. My mother only said that tongues come when you pray and from this point of view, she didn't appear to be praying. At the top of her voice she spoke in another language that I didn't even know either one of us knew, "El demonio menor vivio!' El demonio menor vivio'!"

I glared at Mother Carol with shock. The more I observed her the more I felt terrified of her. She no longer had the loving care of my mother, but of something else. But, when she faced me, she was my mother again. I was speechless and didn't know what happened.

"You understood it didn't you, Gracie?" The figure spoke that was my mother again.

Silently and with total obedience I repeated, "Yes, Mother Carol, you said the demon child lived. The demon child lived."

Mother Carol did not show any emotions, and she did not ask me how I was doing. She only responded in a manner that was truly unlike her, "Rest now, the worse is over and after tonight you won't have to worry again."

The next morning mother was delightful. My body was different in some form, and nothing was out of place. Earlier I wanted to ask her about the baby, but decided not to. She spoke, "Father James will not be back for a while. It will be just the two of us, Gracie."

"Yes, mother," I replied because I knew my father was getting prepared with the rest of the men for battle.

For weeks on end, the last stand was all Majesty Leader spoke of. We all knew our place when the time was given, and I wasn't sure if I wanted to do it. In fact, I wasn't sure of anything anymore. All I knew was what they taught me through the scriptures in the Old Testament. Breaking my thoughts was Mother Carol's soft voice, "As for the child, it will be well taken care of until the appointed time."

"Mother is it my baby?"

"It was never yours, but the enemy."

That was all she said. Over the next three years she and I continued having deeper conversations about destroying the works of the enemy and that was it. Services were the same and life was back to normal. One day before evening service, Mother Carol stood on the garret and faced the half-peeked sun on this cloudy day. The wind blew relentlessly as the air was cooling down.

I looked at her and she had her eyes closed, but she was smiling. That was the first time that I had seen the presence of peace upon her. Easing back into the room, I went to get dressed because that day was the day. I came outside and we went to the ceremony room.

All the men wore their tradition sack cloth, the warrior boys wore head covering, and the women and girls had on our best pilgrimage dresses.

No one spoke, as we walked in through the narrow door. Women and girls of my age were given a cup by the Orders as we were placed to the left of the large circle. I had to be in the back with my mother because of our ranking, in their God. The older men were to the right of the circle and the protectors, our warriors were in the middle. I scanned the crowd to see my brothers, but they all looked alike. I didn't even see Father James and that made me sorrowful. The Orders dimmed the light, and then a bright light shone on the middle of the large circle.

Uncovering his head was the Majesty Leader. He appeared older, but still as handsome as ever to me. For a brief second, I smiled on the time I had with him for no other girl in the compound ever been with him, after me. He spoke, "Today you all will witness the New Era of your salvation. You will be joined in heaven with our father and no more sin!"

Moments later the Orders brought out a small frail child. He appeared to be no more than three. He had a small white drapery on him as he sat on the sacred alter. Majesty Leader spoke with pride and joy, "This is the New Era and by this blood you will rejoice and live forever. Our word tells us a child is born a son is given. Here is our child, here is our son and here he is given to us."

The short Order gave the child a drink and laid the child down. About ten minutes passed and another Order picked up his arms. The child was asleep. I could not tell if he was dead, but either way the sacrifice has to go on. The tallest of the Order's nodded to the

Majesty Leader as he placed containers by the child.

The Order walked off as Majesty Leader began speaking in the same language my mother spoke, but I understood it in English as, "This blood is Holy and undefiled. We give him to you God. Accept him as we partake in his life."

With swift cuts, to the child's neck, wrist, and vein in the leg, he began to bleed into the small containers. It was gruesome and sadly as I cried for the child he offered up for our sins. The more his blood ran they filled the containers up. Majesty Leader blessed the blood by saying, "This life he loses is for us to gain our eternal passage to heaven."

The Orders removed the containers of blood and precede to lite the child's body on fire. The scent of burning flesh overpowered the room. It stunk. Majesty

Leader said loudly, "Molech this offering is to you. We offer up a child for you in your honor."

The Orders gave directions for everyone to bring their cups forward to receive their gift of eternal life. It doesn't feel right to me. I looked over at my mother and she had a dark expression on her face; therefore, it must not be right to her either. I couldn't imagine drinking fresh blood from an innocent child. The way the body was laying with his black curly hair and no life, I felt relieved when someone yelled out, "The invaders are here!"

That meant the women were to run to the inside shelter and drink the special drink while the male fought for our way of life. Mother Carol and I took off with the other women and girls, but we did not go in the room with them. In the mist of the commotion no one saw her snatch my hand to guide me to another passage.

I didn't know what was going on and I never knew that part existed. For a long time, we ran in this dim lit underground muddy clay passage.

When we made it to the end, I saw a wooden door. It was almost like that in my dream, but smaller and without the blood and white ceiling. Mother Carol took out a key from within her apron. Her hands were shivering as she fumbled to unlock it. Soon as the lock fell to the ground, she pushed the door. We jumped outside to roaring thunder and lightning that lit up the night. For the first time, in my life I saw what the outside world looked like. Many people had spoken of what they thought, but there I was actually seeing it.

My mother looked around and so did I. She must have decided on which way to go as she placed her hands on my shoulders and gave me a stare that I would never forget. I stared back with so many

70

questions on my mind. Before I could ask anything, I heard a loud boom from behind me. I jerked around and saw blazes in a distance. Smoke began to fill the tunnel as it oozed out the open door. I saw matching fire coming all from all sizes. This blaze appeared to make the woods to be on fire. I didn't know why the very place I called home was shining bright as flames. However, Mother did not pay any attention to it as my heart was all over my chest.

Mother took out running into the night and I went behind her as fast as I could. It became hard to keep up as it began to misty rain. Lighting lit the sky again as she stop to catch her breath. Before I could say anything, she stated out of breath, "Always believe Jesus and from this point on, if you look back you will be like lot's wife that turned to a pillar of salt. Do you hear me, Gracie? Do you hear me?"

Sensing the urgency in her tone I nodded yes very fast. I remembered the story all too well and she needed not to worry. I was not going to look back. She scanned the sky and I felt afraid because every day since I have been born, I had ever known was church life, God's Word and sacrificial offerings. I began to weep for the uncertainty. Mother Carol saw the direction she wanted to go as she started to race again without looking back at me. Being obedient, I did not look behind me. We did not let up.

Our pace was stronger than before as we went farther away from our everyday life. We would bend over and take in breaths, but that was short. We had to go on. For some reason, she acted like we had to be somewhere at a certain time. I didn't understand why the hurry, but she is mother and God gave her to me; therefore, I have to trust her. The more the lightning struck the brighter the dark night was. When the light was bright, my mother would look for some type of clue. Then, we would take off in whatever direction she felt we needed. I had no idea where we were, but my mother did.

She bent over and placed her hands on her stomach and cried out in pain. Mother Carol fell to her knees in agony. I ran over to touch her, but somehow, she knew I was coming. Therefore, she held her hand up to stop me. I froze in place, not moving because I was not disobedient. She took out gathered her breath and began running with me behind her. Not once did I let her out my sight. That time when she stopped and caught her breath, she looked up at the sky as for some type of sign as to which way to go.

Never again did she look at me and never once did she say anything to me. Now I am disorganized in my thoughts and feelings. Everything was happening to me at once and mother is not telling me anything. Once the thunder roared in our ears, a small white building was in sight. We stop running. She cried out again in a tongue that I never heard of before. To me the language sounded, angry and vengeful. Mother's breathing was rapid, but she swallowed, and her breathing became normal. She fixed her wet dress and smoothed her hair back from under her bonnet. With one profound sigh, Mother Carol opened the double doors, walked into this large old building with me with her.

The room was filled with worn pews and dark brown carpet was on the floor. *Why Mother bring us to a church, in the middle of nowhere and with only a few people here?* I thought. Still not talking to me, she steered me from behind her so I could walk between the pews first with her sitting on the outside. The thunder crackled louder than it did when we ran and it bothered me. This time when the thunder went boom lightning lit up the window we were sitting. I looked outside and saw trees with no leaves. The rain that was misty became thicker. The man who must be the leader spoke, "The devil is real. The lake of fire is real, and the advisory is real as the air you breathe."

I turned my head back at mother as we sat on the back bench. From this angle, she was staring straight ahead, not budging but rigid. It was like she was waiting on someone to help her or go over to her, but no one did anything. I thought again about what the man said about Hell. I wanted to know the answer because in all her teachings, we only spoke of heaven. I whispered, "Mother he is speaking of the faith as we know it?"

She did not say a word, and she still has not look at me. Mother Carol continued to face the front. I don't think she was listening, for her posture was screaming help me, someone please help me now. I didn't know what to think or do. Wanting to get her attention, I tugged on her dress. When I felt her skin, I could not believe how hot she was. I stared at her wanting to know what was going on through her mind; however, she did not budge. The leader said, "You see I know the devil when I see it. I know he comes in many forms and purity is his favorite. If you don't have the Spirit of God, you won't be able to see him for who he really is because you will see what you want. He is a sheep in wolf's clothing."

I glimpsed at mother. Before I could pay more attention to him, she turned her head and faced me. I did not know what to think. She had the appearance of

76

something that was not right. Mother's face was no longer beautiful but lined with craters of wrinkled, red and dark lines. Mother's eyes were sunken so far into their sockets, that shadowy holes were seen. Her ears were pointed with dark spots all over them. The thing must have felt my alarm for it smiled. Its teeth were long, crooked, and decayed in form. The breath from the thing was that of many skunks.

I could not say a word. I did not trust myself to breathe. When it touched me with its' roasting hot hands, I screamed with no sound. I don't see how they don't see what I see. How could these people stand there and let this monster kill my mother from the inside. A tear escaped my eye for I realized that my mother is no more. It leaned closer to my small, panic stricken face. The creature stuck its tongue out and I gasped. My eyes could not get off the tongue in her mouth. It was unnatural with a split that had a hook shape. I was afraid to move my eyes as the monster spoke, "What's wrong my daughter?"

I could not say anything. It put its face inches from mine, flicked the hook tongue and scraped my cheek. I still did not move. It stated, "You see something you recognize?"

Before I could answer, the preacher and the Elders of the church had us surrounded. Mother faced them as they chanted loudly, "The Blood of Jesus is against you Satan. The Blood of Jesus is against you Satan. You have no power, no authority and no dominion here!"

The preacher began to denounce the evil spirit, "You evil spirit come out the woman and go to the pits of Hell, in the name of Jesus!"

The monster began to wail and squirm. The wailing was familiar because I had heard that sound in my dreams many times. The preacher spoke it again this time with more authority. "You stronghold demon, loose this woman in the name of Jesus by the blood of the lamb and return to Hell whence you belong!"

This unknown lady tried pulling me back. I tried reaching for what I thought could still be mother as I yelled out, "Mother, Mother."

Whoever she is, she gave me a small cross from around her neck and spoke, "She is no longer your mother. Her soul is with the devil, and a strongman has taken over her."

At that point, Mother was in the air with more of the front of her body facing me. My Mother had levitated near the ceiling as her body spun in a fast circular motion. I could not believe it. The more her body twisted and jolted, the more she seemed to grow or maybe sprout. She increased in size, muscles, and weight as her clothes fell from her. She was supposed to be naked, but it is not her body I saw. She had no skin, but a hard looking covering with black veins crawling all over her. Her feet were not as a human. They were as two huge hands placed together. Her toes were massive claws, and they curved over like an eagle.

Words could not describe what my mother looked like. This new skin had a fiery appeal that has square shapes. Oddly enough, each square has a big black dot, and the dots had an eye that opened up and bled red blood. I had not seen such a thing in my life. Her once beautiful hair was a deep, flaming red. Her hands had no fingers, but sharp razors and mini razors on each razor. I saw something moving behind her. Suddenly there it was. Swaying back and forth was a long gray tail that bushed red hair at the end. The lady tried to shield my eyes, but I pulled her hands back for I was amazed just like they were of the sight.

Never in my eleven years had I seen or heard of such a sight. The people at the church continued their words at mother. That time one said, "Go back to the pits of Hell Satan, where you belong in the name of Jesus."

When he spoke Jesus name, Mother began to hiss like a snake striking as she slithered closer to the man that spoke the name of Jesus. Once the limbs hit the floor, this thing stood about ten feet high and about four feet wide. I immediately put my hands to my ears because the sound was awful by itself. The thundering became prevalent as the lights flicked. This thing spoke, "Go on quote how you have to have God in you. You all have no power over me. You are weak, pathetic, and you all shall die and come to Hell with me this day."

"We rebuke you! Right now, in the name of Jesus by the Blood of the Lamb."

Mother let out a hideous laugh. When the thunder clapped, lightening shot through the building, and the lights went off. The floor of the building shook and piercing sounds sliced through the air were all around me. People hollered and screamed. I was afraid as I stood there by the other window, not moving. The lady arms did not leave me. She tightens her hold on me. In my ear, I could hear this lady's inaudible, but nervous voice, "Let's pray. Jesus you are in heaven, YOUR name is holy and in YOUR name we are protected by YOUR blood. Help us this day and forgive us of our sins," and that was all I heard her say because her arms tore from me as it ripped the top of my dress.

I didn't know what to do. I could not save the people, even if I tried. My mind could not comprehend what it all meant and what all went on for that matter. I only stood there with the echo of thundering filling the building as I heard glass break. Just like that, the hollering stopped, a funny smell occurred and it was suddenly windy. The lights wink then came back on. My pupils had to gotten larger to take in the sight. Blinking my eyes, I turned my head to and from and I saw no one standing but me.

Everywhere people once stood was a slain body in its place and Mother was gone. The lady that comforted me was to the side with her heart snatched out her chest. The leader's body was spewing blood for the head and neck was missing. But, I did not get disgusted until I saw his hands were missing and the bible he once held was in flames. The other men and women that once surrounded my Mother where cut in pieces. Blood and body parts were all over the place. That was a scene like no other. I reached up to wipe my face for it felt wet.

My mouth flew open because I wanted to holler. I twisted my hands front and back and noticed that I was bloody all over. I repeatedly tried to wipe my hands clean from the blood, but it only made a mess. My eyes became widen with panic as fright clutched my heart. I in my shocking state was numb. When the doors of the church burst open, lightning flashed. A quick view showed a woman standing in a black dress with her back turned. Each time the lightning flashed, I noticed she was twisting my way. Once the thunder clapped, she removed the bonnet and blood dripped everywhere. I could not foresee who it was, but I began to quiver and wipe my eyes. She opened her mouth and yelled, "GO NOW!"

When I did not move, black birds began to fill the place. They started pecking on the dead flesh of the people on the floor. Thunder clasp and lightning flashed again. The figure was gone. I glared all around me and hollered and shook. A familiar smell of burning skin crossed my nostrils as it filled the building. My mind was frantic as I began stepping over the dead bodies to make my way to the door. I didn't know what to do. The building was engulfed with flames. I was scared and nowhere to go, I took out running into the night.

With the rain and wind pressing against me, I jotted through the unknown territory as the sound of dogs barking pierced my ears. I didn't know I could do it, but I ran far and fast. I became tired and sat on the cold icy ground under a tree. My dress was torn, bloody, and dripping wet. My face was drenched with tears and rain; although, the wind blew harder and I shook viciously in the night air. I kept hearing, Jesus will never leave you alone. Jesus is the same every day, all day. Ask HIM to lead you, ask HIM to guide you. Refusing to have the ruling spirit of fear overtaking me, I quickly remembered how God showed Moses where to take the people.

I also remembered that God's Spirit lives in me and it would lead and guide me. I was no longer afraid, but encouraged to leave the woods and just like God did Abraham towards a strange land. I know he will provide a way for me to come out alive. Loud noises lead me straight ahead, so I ran to the sound. When I exploded out the woods, I saw a hard looking road. At this point, I am bedazzled and distraught. A thing with lights passed me by. Once it was gone, I remembered someone calling it a car. As if it was predestine, the next car stopped. A tall older man got out of the car with an older, smaller, but thin woman. They both have gray hair and you can tell that years are upon them; however, their appearance was familiar. The woman placed her jacket around me, and they put me in their car. They drove without saying a word and I in return did not either.

They did not ask any questions as we rode in silence. I was afraid in a way, but that felt right. I am in a strange thing among strange people, but it did not feel as foreign to me. I am for the first time, seeing new sights and that were terrifying. Upon making it to their home, we sat in the driveway. I had no idea what they were thinking, and I had no idea what was in store, but I believed that is meeting is of God because my spirit did not feel troubled. The man turned towards me and spoke first, "I am Minister Gabriel McBride, but everyone calls me Minister Gabe. This is my wife Tammy Mae, but we all call her Tillie. What is your name?"

Looking up at them made me feel safe. I gathered my voice and spoke, "Grace. My name is Grace."

"Do you have a last name Grace?"

"I don't know it. Girls only used first names."

"When you say we, what do you mean?"

"I was with Mother Carol, and we are a part of the compound that was taken over by the invaders tonight."

I could not go on and speak of my mother because I don't know what really has become of her. Therefore, I froze. They noticed that I choked. Mrs. Tillie softly said, "Its okay. You are safe now and you are welcome to stay here for the night and tomorrow when we all talk."

I nodded my head, and we got out. I could not see the entire beauty for it was dark and foggy. Mr. Gabe opened the door, and I got out. Mrs. Tillie unlocked their door, and we went inside. The front room was wonderful, and a lot of pictures were hanging all around. I have only heard of such a home, but to actually see it was different.

"You hungry, Gracie?"

"No Ma'am, just cold and tired."

"Ok. Come with me."

She directed me down the hall and showed me the bathroom. It was bright and warm. The way it was decorated, made me feel better. Minutes later, she came back and gave me some clothes.

"I don't think you wear pants, so I brought you this night gown to sleep in."

"Thank you."

I ran the water and stepped into the tub. The water was wonderful as it waved to and fro against my skin. The soap she had smelled different, sweeter to be exact. I lathered up and did not want to get out. I hadn't had a bath like that since, I left Majesty Leader's house. I frown for I thought of all the night's events. Once I finished, she came back in showed me to the room where I was to sleep. She turned lights on, and said, "Here is the room. I hope you like it." I walked in the room and twirled around for it was magnificent. It was one that Mother Carol had mentioned before. I always thought that it was a metaphor, but there I was looking at her words come to pass. Mrs. Tillie asked, "I take it you like it?"

"Yes, I do."

"Great. My husband and I will be down the hall if you need us."

"Thank you so much."

"Great, we will talk in the morning."

I only nodded and she left out. Going to the big bed I sat there and realization hit me. I was alone. My brothers died along with Father James. My mother was no longer my mother, but a demon spirit. Just the thought of what my mother looked like gave me chills. Yarning, I removed the covers and got into bed. *She called me Gracie*, I thought as I laid there in bed. Deciding not to linger more, I closed my eyes and went to sleep.

All in my sleep, I could see was the evil creature my mother had turned into. My eyes could not believe the transformation. No matter how I tried to fight the images, I saw and heard of nothing else. I often weep for the lost souls that tried to cast out the devil in my mother, but had no avail. The way everything was it made my future bleak. For months, I was in a semi-life state. I ate and bathe, but did no interactions. The McBride's did not pressure me and that was great. They were nice and kind and for that I was very grateful.

However, that did not stop me from being depressed and oppressed by spirits as I battled my inward war. It seemed hard to pray and harder to think, but somehow, I knew I had to snap out of it and move forward. Jesus was with me and that was more than any family. As if a light came on in my head, I felt the presence of God with me. I suddenly had peace that surpassed my understanding and was confident in going to do battle with the enemy. I knew that day was the day I must put an end to the sorrowful spirit.

I put on the clothes she had set aside for me and prayed. I made the bed up for that was the only thing that needed cleaning. Soon as I finished a light knock was heard, and then the voice, "Gracie, you woke? It's me, Mrs. Tillie."

"Come in."

She came in looking radiant as she asked, "Would you like to come downstairs?"

I smiled and walked behind her. We made it to the spacious kitchen and on the table were pancakes, eggs, orange juice, and fresh peeled oranges. My stomach growled and I sat down. Mr. Gabe began to bless the food, like Father James use to do before he had to do more duties on the other side. Mr. Gabe stated, "So, Grace, the spirit of God tells me that you are ready to talk?"

My mouth became locked as I stopped chewing because my spirit agreed with him. I knew they needed to know because they have been good to me. Swallowing, I sat back, and spoke, "I don't know if you would believe me. If I had not have been there, I would not believe it. But, everything is real, and I witnessed it."

Mr. Gabe looked at me, and said, "Let us pray before we talk any further." We all bowed our heads, and he prayed, "We come before you Lord, broken and confused. Close our natural minds and open our spiritual minds, so that we may hear what the spirit is saying. In your name Jesus, we pray Amen, Amen." Everyone said Amen, and then he spoke on, "Grace, if it's to any comfort we will believe you. Many people do not believe that there is a world here that exists within the world we live in." I was puzzled as he said,

94

"We can see the houses, cars, and trees, but what we can't see is evil or good until it's used by someone. We can't even see hatred or love for that matter until someone shows it."

I smiled for I knew he understood. Taking a sigh, "I don't know why, but I am compelled to tell you that I saw evil in its purest form, and it was in the body of Mother Carol."

When I spoke that, I waited on them to say something or do something, but they did neither. They had their attention focused on me, but Mrs. Tillie had tears in her eyes. I said, "I am from the compound that believes in the New Era, but my mother didn't teach me their ways. It was like she was two different people. In front of them I had to know the ways that Majesty Leader showed, but when it was just the two of us, it was all Jesus. I had the feeling that she was trying to

95

protect me and hurt me all at the same time, but I don't know why."

"She was playing both sides," Mr. Gabe spoke.

"Listen to the last line in each Verse. According to JOB 1:14-19, it talks about how Job lost everything and everything was going against him. It talks how in every situation Job was in, someone was left to tell what happened, and when losing cattle and servants did not bother him. His most prize possessions were taken, his children. Also, when they were gone, there was someone to tell what happened to them." They still did not respond so I spoke, "If you want to see a miracle, look at me. I only am a survivor in a spiritual fight. I only am escaped to tell thee."

Mrs. Tillie had tears in her eyes, and said, "We believe you and there are some things we must tell you."

She glanced up at Mr. Gabe and he gave her the go head. Placing her hand on mine, like Mother Carol use to. I with tears in my eyes waited for her to speak. She whispered in a tone that was familiar, "We know all about it. We needed for you to trust us enough to tell us."

I stared at them and remembered that is why they look familiar to me. I have been with them before, but don't really remember when it happened. I looked at her and Mr. Gabe spoke, "Please, don't think unkind of us, but it was no mistake that we were there that night. Carol got word to us that it was out of her control and no matter what, we were to get you and protect you, with all cost. Where she failed, she needed you to be strong and do what is called for you to do."

"So is that why she was teaching me all about Jesus?"

Mrs. Tillie spoke, "Partial. Jesus is the only God and she needed to teach you the truth so you would not go to Hell. The next part is, Carol told us that you believe in Christ and that you are filled, which is so wonderful."

"Why did she not leave earlier?"

"She desired to leave, but was reluctant to. She thought that it was all her fault, and she so desperately tried to right her wrong. When Carol saw she couldn't do it, she contacted us."

We all did not speak. However, to break the silence Mr. Gabe said, "She wants us to finish teaching you the pure unadulterated Word of God so you can wax strong. Whatever it is, it is mighty, but the Spirit of God can triumph over anything. Now you are filled, Gracie, you must learn to operate in the Spirit."

"How do you know Mother Carol?"

Mrs. Tillie, gave my hand a slight squeeze, and spoke, "Carol is our only child."

"You mean you are my grandparents?"

"Yes, we are."

I looked to each one, and then said, "You mean I have family in the Truth?"

"Yes, Gracie, you do."

Mrs. Tillie got up and gave me a wholesome hug. It was wonderful to feel the love just by a hug. Mr. Gabe then got up, and said, "We love you, Gracie. We have always loved you and have kept you all in prayer."

"Tell me about how Mother Carol got to the compound."

"This is a Christian household, and we were strict on her because of the evil of this world, but she had her own mind. We made it our business to teach her Jesus and that was all we could do. She met James, your

99

father, at a church meeting. He was from that horrible place and our daughter fell madly in love with him. She wanted to marry him, but we would not allow it. She was too young and impressionable. She ran away from here and we never saw her again until she was pregnant with you. It is then we learned of the lifestyle. Our daughter told us she sold her soul to the devil because of love. She said she later repented, but she couldn't leave her husband and her children. However, Carol told us that she had a vision that the devil was in her like never before and how she was having a girl child. The child must preach the Word and when the time comes to do what she must."

"Do what?"

"We don't know that, but what we do know is that you must believe Jesus is your Lord and Savior."

"I do."

"From the firmness in her voice, she knew that what happened at that church was to occur."

When they mentioned the church, I felt afraid and began crying hysterically. All I have ever known was lost and nice people are more than likely in Hell. They both came to me and tried to soothe me. They didn't witness what I did and they don't know how my mother appeared to me and how blood was everywhere.

"Shush, Gracie it's going to be ok. Christ had you to witness that, but it is to make you stronger. You had to see that because what is to come is going to be worse."

"You don't know how Mother Carol looked when that thing took over her. You don't know how it was to be the only survivor covered in blood. I won't forget it any of it."

"Carol would not tell us more. We don't know the magnitude of it all, but we know that when you brought forth the child."

"That was my son that Majesty Leader sacrificed to Molech?" I said with faint.

"You didn't know?" My grandmother spoke softly.

"I felt a connection to the child, but was unaware that he was mine, from my loins. Oh God help me!"

I began to cry all the more. Nothing they said could help me because I saw the way the enemy destroyed my son. His own father performed the ceremony. When I think about it I would cry out to the Lord, and I wept sore. Before I knew what was happening. I activated the Holy Spirit in me. I cried out, stomped my feet, and spoke in an unknown tongue. It was not like the way the Spirit came inside me the first time. It was more advanced.

They had to move me away from the table. Nothing could help. I was there to witness the slaying of the child. I knew, but didn't really know he was mine. I had forgot all about the child, for I was a child my own self. When I opened my eyes, my grandparents were there. I sat up some and they smiled. I knew they'd never leave my side.

"You became slain in the spirit."

My grandfather brought me a cup of water, and spoke, "We can't imagine what you are feeling, we can only guess. Carol loved you and from what we know she sheltered you."

"She did."

"Your grandmother and I can't change what happened, but we can do all we can to equip you with the whole armor of God. It's up to you, if you so choose to."

There I was, rambling within my own self as what to do. Mother Carol once told me that when the window of opportunity came, we must know when to walk in it and not doubt. Listening to the Spirit of God in me, I glanced in their direction and spoke, "I do humbly accept Jesus's Will for my life, and I will do all within my power to destroy the work of the enemy."

"Gracie, it will not be easy because we will be drilling you about the Word of God, fasting, praying, and taking on speaking engagements to tell the people about the enemy."

"The enemy took my life and now I must return the favor with Christ as my backbone."

"We are so proud of you. You have no idea how much this means to us. We just wish that Carol could have been here, but we know that she too is in God's plan."

"May I ask a question?"

"Go ahead child."

"What happened to my mother after she turned into the evil thing?" They both paused as if to think of what to tell me. I stated, "My mother taught me that in the King James version that is usually translated by some phrase such as to be possessed, or to be vexed, by demons or evil spirits. Either way, it doesn't matter what has happened to her, I will understand in time."

My grandparents placed me in my mother's old room and over all I was glad. I learned more about my mother than I had all my life. They are truly hard and great stewards in God's Word, and I can see why mother ran off. They weren't mean, but stern when it came to the things of God. Every day I studied my home school work and God's Word. There wasn't time to play around for defeating the enemy was not a joke.

Sure, we had laughs like others, but they were all short lived when it came to my lessons. We had Wednesday's set aside for fasting and praying. I literally ate, drank, and breathed Jesus Christ and the cross. The good part was, I didn't mind. I know I have a destiny to do and that made me more joyful. I took their last name and that was right. My senses in the Lord were great, and they were right, it was not easy; however, I have a humble spirit and that made it easier.

To be as young as I was, the gifts of the Spirit were abundant in my life. The Lord showed favor on me by opening my mind of understanding and wisdom. I was truly a Son of God, a Daughter of Zion a World Deliverance Minister, when it came to HIS Word. Whenever I needed something for the Lord all I had to do was ask and it would be done. When I pray people were healed and when I preached people were delivered all because of the faith.

I too liked other people in God, and I had to deal with many things. It was not a cake walk, and it was not an easy life, but a life worth living. At the age of twenty, my life took a toll when both my grandparents went on to be with the Lord at once. They taught me that to always use the KJV as they called it. It's the King James Version. I was to use it and back up anything I had to say from it for it was the only true Holy Word of God Himself. The scriptures were as God breathes.

My grandparents taught me all they could, but they could not explain the nightmares that still plagued me off and on. The last thing grandma Tillie told me was that the enemy would come at me the more powerful I become in God. She also stated that Lucifer the devil only wants to steal, kill, and destroy any positive future I would have. With tears in her eyes that day, she spoke more earnest as she squeezed my hand with love.

I didn't know what to think. All my life they have been preparing me for the work of God and that was it. I knew she told me that my demons were coming, and I better be in a place with God that Satan himself must ask for permission. In all honesty, I know that JOB had been one of those men and for her to tell me that was almost farfetched. It threw me back, when I became alone again in this cruel world, but it did not stop me. It only made me fierce in the Word and increased my faith. Not only did I believe Jesus, but I knew that he answers me when I pray. Even when I would think of Christ would not use me anymore, I would think about others who died in the faith and their downfall. Paul killed Christians, Mosses hit the rock, David committed adultery, Martha worried, Mary Magdalene was a whore, and Thomas doubted God. Surely the Lord used them, he could and still would use me.

Twenty-Five Years Later

I had never thought about getting married and one day I went to preach at Cotton Grove Jesus Applied Pentecostal Church of God In Christ. The Lord spoke, "The man that comes to you and give you the scripture First Corinthians eleven and one, Follow Christ as I follow Christ, he is to be your husband. You have been alone long enough. The time has come for you to be submissive to a husband that will love you."

I stopped dead in my tracks. I have not been touched by any man since my youth and my entirety has been a devout Christian, spreading the Word of God to churches throughout the world. I heard that I had a husband in the building. I have not ever focused on a man, men in general. A husband was the last thing I needed. My mind became cloudy as I scanned the crowd. I did not see any men since it was a woman's retreat at a church. For the first time in a long time, I wanted to believe that God has made a mistake. I thought, *A husband on a woman's retreat, for real?*

When I saw that I questioned God I quickly repented and forgot about it. I made it to the platform and prayed over the Word. Soon as I scanned the crowd, the Holy Ghost spoke, "The head is sick, the body is dying. The marriage is in ICU."

I stood there after prayer and observed the crowd again. My spirit felt the great cry from these women. I know they are wondering why I did not speak, but I listened to my spirit. When I opened up my mouth I spoke, "Women, Praise God. I plan to speak to you about your marriage, the head and the body."

I was quiet because the Lord was speaking to me, and HE said, "ICU, marriages need to be helped and healed."

Taking a sigh of, Lord have your way, I spoke with assurance, "Before I get started bare with me. I will be going back and forth saying, Jesus says, Peter says and so on. Ok, marriages are in ICU. This is what God revealed to me about the head and the body. I thought it would consist of scriptures that would have pointed the finger, but it did not. ICU is a state of unconscious when something is wrong and the body is unaware of what is going on. During this time the body will have reflexes, but still be unaware of what is really happening. Man is the head of the woman, and the woman is the body. Damage may be in the body, but it starts in the head. The head must respond before the body can move. The body does what the head wants it

112

to do. Without the head the body is lifeless and unresponsive to what is going on. There are times the eyes may flicker, the body will open their eyes, but it still can't do much until the head sends signals that it can do so. When going through we want to give up. In some cases give up and die. Mark 14:27-38 states how Jesus is saying the head of the body will be wounded and the family will go astray. If the head of the body, family, is not operating as it should the family, body, won't be able to respond as it should. If HE takes away the head then the body will be in a semi-life form unable to nothing, but to flicker, wonder, and make jerking movements because of the head is out of whack. He tells them it is because of me so I being the head shall go first. Here Peter, the body said, no matter what the head says I will be able to respond, and I will recover. I will still be here able to move able to do what

I need to do. Jesus, the head said. I was the head I knew how the body would respond. You say what you want, but I know what you will do. I know what you are going to do. Peter, the body, said I will try to fight to live, I will wiggle, I will try to open my eyes, I will somehow move my fingers, squeeze a hand just to live, but if what you are saying is true, then before I try to live without you and be in a coma then I will die. I will give up and die because the head is dead. Here Jesus is saying, Right now I need you the body to still be aware, still be here, still be able to move while I, the head, get looked at so I can make you move, but for now it is on me. Jesus told the body what was going to happen and when HE felt that some parts of the body is going to need more work. Peter is the rock, James is the other parts that are important, and John the heart. Jesus began to feel the body was dying in some form. He knew the

114

body needed work, but could not function until the head responds. Jesus is saying the head has to be seen and I need the body more active parts to be ready to move and be waiting so when the time is right, we will all move. The head is thinking well I want to live so it moved. When the head thinks about falling it shows that everything starts there. Is the body worth it? Am I worth it? Since the body wants to live and I feel like I want to live let me think about it and kind of weigh the options. Here Jesus, the head, wants to give up. HE did not want the body to suffer anymore HE did not want to do what HE wanted to do. Just like us, situations comes upon us and we often times make up our minds to let it go, give up because we can't take what is happening in the body and the body has tried to move, but deep down knows it needs the head, but in the this state the head knows it needs help far more than it realized because not only were their lives at state, but others that depended on it to live. If the body was not important it would have completely shut down without tarring. Even though, Jesus knew that being the head was hard, HE knew that the body would not be able to handle HIS ways alone. HE wanted to feel the release and not go through what was ahead of HIM. HE prayed to do what was needed because in HIS mind HE knew how the body was suffering without HIM. HE knew what needed to be done but didn't want to do it. The head knows what the body needs therefore the head has to be clear. It cannot think about what is best for them because there are other parts that deserve to move even if it doesn't want to move. If Jesus wanted to give up when HE became heavy grieved, hurt by life, and things in it, then what are we? Again, Jesus, the head, said to Peter to the body who is also the determination,

116

the force the will I'm clear I'm thinking again I decided that I want to you to live. I am here. The head is also saying now I know what I need to do and that is be strong and do what is necessary for my body to make it. The head realized that it is not all about him it was about everything connected to him that he needed to function again as a unit a whole. When the head made up its mind to do what it needed the body took another turn went to sleep because it had decided to let go because it got tired of waiting on the head to wake up, got tired of saying, I moved and you didn't move, I showed you that I'm here and yet you still didn't want to do what you needed to do so we can get up from this state, it said, Head I'm done let me be let me sleep, let me be unaware of what is going on. Jesus is saying we are together again, we are going to come out this and we are going to move. We are going to get out this bed

117

and stay focus on how not to be found not knowing what is needed of us. It was never about the body it was about the head lining up to make the body move for the head is the beginning. Jesus is saying, if we don't do what we need to do, stay guarded, be discerning of snares, traps, bonds, ties the enemy will find a way to temp us. If you a diabetic too much sugar, high blood pressure too much pork, jesting too much talking, the enemy will have you to doubting if the head and if the body wants to live again. Everything starts with a thought, and everything starts in the head. The head may not let on to the body that something is wrong and when it doesn't the body becomes damage and is need of fixing because it didn't know what the head was thinking the cells can't start the repairing process. Here Jesus is saying, do what you need to do. It is that moral feeling you feel when you do what is right. You may

118

not want to do it because it is who we are, but it is no longer about two things, it is about one and that is the body being fit, being made over and being on one accord. We may not do what we need to do, but it's on the inside of you because it's bigger than you. The head need its body, and the body needs its head, together it can get up and be strong and stand anything that comes their way only if they are doing what is needed. Catch phrase is, you are weak in your skin. Here Jesus is saying I, the head, got weak, but I went to the higher power and got strengthen. Now I am no longer concerned about how I feel about things, it's not about me anymore, its bout my body too how my body needed me and how I wasn't there and when I needed my body it wasn't there. They didn't operate together, and they got out of line and found themselves in a bed with one trying to do without the other but I don't work

119

that way. Now they are together again be strong and not weak because if they don't they will get derailed and find themselves back in another situation because they didn't stand together. They can't go back, but if they don't kill out what they want or want to do, how they feel or what they think. They will be doomed, that is why when people go through so much staying sick, depressed, lonely, tired, you can see the giving up, and before you know it they are dead. They could not handle it because the head and the body did not stay connected, they did not stay connected to Jesus. If the body and the head do not line up it will not stay in sync it will fall back into temptation and eventually find itself dead in that bed, which it lies. Women, continue to uplift your husband in prayer. Continue to do what you have too because in due season, the head will wake up."

The women were clapping and some even shouted, but nonetheless it is God's Word and the Holy Ghost had HIS way. I walked back from the podium, kneeled and prayed for a moment. Once the speaking engagement was over, I was about to leave until the Bishop of that area came to me. He is tall, with salt and pepper hair and the most stunning creature I had ever seen. I liked his smile and the first thing he told me was, "I am lead to tell you that you need to follow me as I follow Jesus."

Ever since then he and I have not be separated. We dated for five months before marriage. His deceased wife Marsha, son Daniel and Daniel's wife Carry died three years before in a car wreck. The twins Daniel Jr. and Carla Ann had to be delivered by cesarean. He has partial custody of them along with his son's wife's mother Anna and that weekend they would come to the house for a visit. *No more quiet time until they leave,* I thought as I began to think about my loving husband.

Just thinking about how blessed I was to have William. He was someone I could talk to and no matter how I felt he understands me. When I fell down, he knew just what to say and for the majority we always finish each other's sentences. The best thing was we both were in God and we were almost like other married couples. The difference is we both know God and we know that God is a God of divine order and anything else is of the enemy. We have our differences like ordinary people and we for the most are happy.

A knock came to the door and I quickly remembered that William brought me something as always. With a caring smiled, I replied, "Come in."

He came through the door carrying a snack tray with a rose.

"My darling, you are so wonderful" I spoke with admiration.

"What less would you expect of me?" He asked with that smile of his.

"I don't."

He leaned towards me and we gave a slight peck on the lips. He said, "You do need to eat something light."

At that moment my stomach growled. We laughed. "Well God is an on time, God."

"And, God knows it is time for you to eat."

With tender laughing and warm smiles, I spoke, "Lets' go to the kitchen nook."

He turned around and I followed him to the nook. We ate tuna sandwich, an apple, and drank some water. We chatted for a spell longer and that was short lived because time went fast. I left him to clean up the area while I went to get dressed. Later I arrived downstairs and got dressed for that night service. Afterwards, we had to pick up the children.

The ride to the church in William's old district was odd. I always kept it quiet and stayed focused. But, for some reason, we chatted about going on a vacation at the end of summer. The idea does have an appeal to it and I am anxious, but I know the Word told us to be anxious for nothing but somehow, I had the urge to get away with my husband.

We arrived at The Jesus Tabernacle People Incorporated United Way Presbyterian on time. I prayed as always that the Lord allowed me to go into the church and speak as HE would have me. The ministry was like many others that deny the trinity, the

God head, let alone speak in tongue, but the new board wanted something different and asked me to come in because they heard that I didn't take down and I allow God's Will. I was honored and the timing was perfect. My previous engagement had cancelled due to weather.

My husband opened the door for me. I adjusted my cloak and reached for my bible. To meet me was a woman in her mid-twenties. Her skirt was extremely tight as it rose above her knees as her expensive smelling perfume breached my nostrils. She was no doubt over taken with lust and seducing spirits. From the way she walked and from the way she acted I knew the spirits lived in her for a long time. She spoke as she saw me, "Minister Dalton, it is an honor to have you speaking at tonight's message for deliverance. The people need to be free from the traps of the enemy."

"Thank you and I hope you feel the same when they come out of you tonight."

She was stunned from my answer, but that mattered not. I have a job to do and I plan to do it. Without saying anything else, she showed me the small sanctuary for me to pray. I walked in, got comfortable, and anointed my head and ears. For what was hours, I finally got up. I was not exhausted as I usually would be; however, tonight it is to be different. A slight knock was heard, and I opened the door. It was an usher. She handed me a bottle of water and a towel. Before she left, I spoke, "Jesus wants me to tell you that HE loves you even if you are doing that thing that no one knows about, but HIM. HE said to tell you that you asked HIM for deliverance this morning and for me to pray for you, right now."

She began to cry. I normally don't operate in the spirit of the Prophet, but it matters not to me because it was not about me that spoke. Whatever HE told me to tell the people I would, they would like it or not. I would do my job. However, the woman continued to cry. I anointed her head and had her to hold her hands up as a sign to Christ that she surrenders all to HIM. The lady obeyed and I began to pray, but when the spirit of God takes over, it is no longer I that pray, but Holy Spirit within me that pray.

The more God's Spirit spoke the harder she cried. The lady I knew battled alcohol and she did not want anyone to know, but you can't hide anything from Jesus. With her eyes closed, I gathered the small wastebasket and some tissue. I knew her deliverance was coming. Seconds later the lady was spewing up spit and snot out of her mouth. I kept telling her to let it out

127

and didn't stop. Another small knock was at the door, and it was the second Usher. I told her to work with the lady and don't stop until she was filled. The second lady worked with the other Usher, as I got ready to go forth in the Word.

When I made it in the hall, I stopped, and closed my eyes. I heard the Holy Spirit say don't teach on love, teach on if God be with you who can be against you. I spoke loudly, "Thank you Lord."

I walked through the door, and the choir was in the mist of their praise. They were singing their version of "Its Only a Test You're Going Through." I could feel the rush of energy down in my soul as they sung. The presence of the Lord is most definitely here, and I know that the Lord is going to use me. Closer and closer as I walked, chills were all on me and pressing on me to shout. Making it through the small door I joined in their praise ceremony. My feet would not allow me to be still.

I was dancing like never before without further ado, I shouted and praised my Savior like never before. I got my deliverance for Jesus knew when you need to shout, cry, or just move. The people were in no doubt praising God all over the place. With no holding back, the tongues became prevalent as the choir sang the song in parts. The Spirit of God was everywhere. I did as the Spirit of God ordered me to do. I got the oil and laid hands on the people. Many became slain in the Spirit as others cried out, danced, and waved their hands for freedom. When the choir was winding down their song, I paced the floor as I spoke with my headset on, "Hallelujah! Hallelujah! Everyone needs to praise God, for HE is God."

I jumped in one spot like a spring. I pointed to the floor, and spoke, "If you can't praise HIM here." Then I pointed towards the ceiling to represent Heaven, to say, "You can't praise HIM there."

I stopped jumping and spoke in tongues as the Spirit gave me utterance. Once the tongues returned to English, I yelled out to the people, "Colossians one and sixteen talks about how God created everything for HIM and HIS purpose. No matter where the location is, HE created it for HIM, and everything was created by HIM. If HE created you, HE intends to use you. Don't wait until it's too late!" The people praised Christ even more. The drums and guitarist only played as I spoke clearer, "THANK HIM! Thank the Lord of your salvation. Over in Psalm forty-six and one through seven states clear how God is there for you. HE is your protection and no matter how things look in your life, you can always come to HIM for peace, and HE alone will keep you safe. If God be with you, who can be against you? None in the earth, that's who!"

Louder than ever, the people shouted and praised God, even their leader was on his knees crying out. His wife, whom was covered like other women with white sheets, were still slain and allowed Christ to deal with her. I spoke, "Don't keep quiet. Your deliverance is in your praise. Luke nineteen and forty talks about making stones cry out. It says how if the people HE created don't want to praise HIM, HE will find anything to praise HIM. Don't let a rock beat you in praising God. If God be with you who can be against you? If you are in Christ and Christ in you, then you are on the inside looking out! You have no need to worry, stress or become depressed, oppressed, and bound by anything! In fact, Genesis fifty and twenty verifies the devil will take your bad decisions and everything you have done wrong and hold it over your head. But, God Almighty will allow you time to repent and learn from what was bad. Not only that, but give you grace to know that HE loves you, today and every day. Even when you mess up, God will take your mess, and make it whiter than snow. If HE is with you HE is with you. HE doesn't give up, HE gives out. Psalm thirty-seven and twenty-five talks about through life, young and old none of HIS children will beg or be left out."

People ran up and down the aisle to praise Christ all the more. I could only shout as the Word is right all by itself and I heard the Holy Spirit speak, "That is enough."

I went back to my seat and got on my knees as people were still slain in the spirit. I thank God for HIS will being done and not mine. I didn't even have to speak for when the Spirit has its way there is no manner of word that needs to be spoken. I glanced up and the Usher gave me a towel to wipe the sweat from my brow and bottle of water. The pastor of the church got up and said with much enthusiasm, "What a Word from God! Hallelujah!"

He glanced over at me and said, "Minister Dalton, God answers prayers."

He turned his face back to the congregation and spoke, "Now, it is time to take up a special offering for the speaker that allowed Christ to use her mightily. The Word tells us to give, and it shall be given back to us. Not just that, but a worker is worthy, and we must give her our carnal things for she has departed in us spiritual things from God. True manner from on High, is what we all were fed this day."

After they blessed the offering, the pastor dismissed the service. People were still on the floor slain and the way they looked none of them left the same way. I was pleased because you never want to go to service one way and return the same way. Each and every place I spoke, the Lord changed many of them, if not all. In my sight was a little boy with blond hair. He appeared to be about three years old and when he got closer his eyes were familiar. I could not shake the feeling that was all over me. He stopped in front of me and I spoke, "My child where are your parents?"

He handed me a locket and spoke, "Mother, I hope you would tell me."

When he said that, I looked around to see if anyone heard him. Placing my attention back to him and the child was gone. I gasped, but still in my clinch was the locket. Quickly I put the locket away and the pastor disturbed my thoughts by saying, "You alright? You look like you have seen a ghost."

"No I'm fine, just a little tired. I'm sure I don't have to tell you how the preaching can drain you."

"Trust me, I know and after tonight, I know you need to rest." I smiled. He spoke again, "Oh, here is the offering from tonight. You don't know how you have blessed this church body spiritually."

Without reaching for it, I asked, "Could you please have your Treasury Department to take the tenth off for your ministry?"

He was taken by surprise as he said, "I sure can."

He walked off and five minutes later William came over, and asked, "You ok? You were talking to yourself."

Before I could answer, the pastor came back over and handed me another closed envelope.

"Thank you."

"You're welcome."

He turned to my husband and spoke as I listened, "Bishop Dalton you must bless us, as well."

"However, the Lord leads, and we always pray HIS Will."

"Great. I have to go and you both have a safe trip back home."

"We will we have to get the grand babies for the night."

"How are they?"

"They are growing like weeds and darlings as ever. Isn't that right my love?"

"He is right, and we need to go before it gets later than what it is?"

"You right."

My husband turned to the pastor and spoke as they shook hands, "Until we meet again."

"Likewise Bishop."

We left the building and got in the car. William began to drive to toward Anna's house. I had an eerie feeling about it and it started when I saw the little boy after the service. Remembering the incident, I started to reach in for the locket, but didn't.

"So, are you going to tell me what you thought you saw back at the church?"

"I thought I saw a ghost from my past."

"You always amaze me."

Seconds later we pulled up to Anna's house. The police and fire vehicles were there. William jumped out the car and I was behind him. In earshot, I heard my husband ask, "What's wrong?"

"The carbon oxide alarm went off and luckily we came just in time to awaken them."

William and I went toward the children and Anna. They sat in the back of the ambulance.

"We are okay. Thank God."

I went to the children, and they were still sleepy, but the techs spoke that they are alright. William talked to Anna, and she did not appear distraught, but when she placed her head on his shoulders I knew that she was sorrowful. Making my way over to them, William gave me a hug as he whispered, "They said the house is not safe for them to stay. Would it be ok for them to stay a few days with us until it is safe?"

"Oh, my dear, of course it will be ok. They are family. How can I say no?"

William gave me a smile, and then spoke, "Thank you."

We walked together as the techs brought the children over to Anna. William said, "We have discussed it. You and the children can vacation at our house until things here are cleared."

"Bishop, Minister Grace, I can't. I mean we can't impose on your generosity."

"Sister Anna, it is fine. You will not be imposing. Plus, you haven't seen where we live so this will be great for you."

"Come here you two."

Sister Anna gave us a group hug, and it actually felt nice to do something nice for her. Her husband had been dead for ten years and she built her life around her grandchildren. Sister Anna was tall and well built. She didn't look a day over thirty, but she was forty-five. Her hair hangs far past her shoulders and her oval eyes brighten her face when she smiles. I never had a problem with her and have no reason to think I would. She and I talk frequently.

Sister Anna was a loving person and a joy. However, she didn't do much as she used to because she had the children and was a missionary that sat on the church board to one of the biggest churches in her district. Not just that, the woman could sing like an angel and could usher in the Spirit of God at will. The only problem was she can be more powerful if she allows God to move more in her life. A lot of things she says are worldly, but she does not think any different about it. Many times, she has come to me and I did spiritual warfare on her behalf. She would be delivered again and weeks later she would be worse off than she was.

Christ delivering her through me was our personal thing. Not even William knew. I believed she thought he would try to take the children, but that was likely. In fact, it had been a few weeks since her last deliverance and I was glad to see she was still standing. William left us standing alone to go fetch the children. Sister Anna politely touched my arm, and said, "This really means so much to me to have you welcome me as you have."

"Sister Anna, I'm glad you all are ok. As for clothing, don't worry about raiment. I am sure we can get you all something else to wear."

"Minister Grace, it means a lot to me that you open your home to me and my grandchildren under these circumstances. I just can't thank you enough."

Giving her a slight grin I said with a yarn, "Come on let's go. It's getting late."

We walked to the car and William already had the children locked down in the car. She got in the back with the children, and I got back in the front. Time was getting away as William drove, I spoke, "Sister Anna, I don't mean to be rude, but I am exhausted from speaking tonight and I am going to shut my eyes for a little rest."

"That's fine I am going to do the same."

"William, will you be ok, as we sleep?"

"Yeah, babe, I'll be fine. I am not going to fall asleep."

"Ok. I don't want to awake to see Jesus either."

We laughed and I said, "I'm just saying."

"I know you are. I'm just saying tone."

"Well, the last time you said you were awake, I woke up and you started snoring."

"Grace, that was the last time, and I wasn't sleepy; somehow, my eyes closed on their own."

We laughed. I was afraid when he was awake by himself to drive me from a long trip after speaking. I lightly touched his arm. He turned his head and gave me that all too familiar smile of reassurance. My love said, "I have some things on my mind tonight and I could use the quietness."

"Ok, but if you feel like you can't do it, it's ok to wake me."

"I love you Grace."

"Love you too, babe."

I glanced in the rear view mirror and saw that Sister Anna was fast asleep, like the children. Sinking lower into the seat, I closed my eyes and went to sleep.

Phase 2

We made it to the house, and we awoke our visitors. Sister Anna and I each took a child as William unlocked the door.

"Wow, this is such a lovely home you both have."

"Wait until the morning, you haven't seen anything yet."

"William, babe I'm going to show Sister Anna to the guest room."

"If it's ok with you both, I would really like for the children to sleep in the room with me. I don't know if I could part with them tonight."

Feeling the spirit of depression, using wisdom I spoke, "It is fine. We understand the near death experience and would not have it any other way. I think it would be great for the children to be in there with you."

"You are ever so kind."

"I agree with Minister Grace," William said with joy.

I gave her a smile of assurance that we are here for her because I can only imagine the pain and fear she is feeling. She has taken on a great task of raising young children when she could live her life, but instead, she chose a life of being a mother all over again. Giving her one last glance I placed my other hand on her and spoke sweetly, "Come this way with me." I showed her to the guest room and when I turned the light on she was amazed for I saw it on her face. I placed Carla Ann on the bed and she placed little Daniel on the other side. Going over to the closet, I handed her a gown, and stated, "I know it is a little short, but you are taller than me, but it will be good enough to sleep in for now."

"Thank you."

"You're welcome and good night."

I went upstairs to retire for it was a little after two in the morning and that night the moon was bright as it lit up my bedroom. I closed my eyes as I lain in bed beside William thinking, *how I have built my life around the Word of God and my marriage. I would do anything I could to protect him, but who is going to protect me from my mind? Where can I be safe?* Before I could rationalize my thoughts further, something pressed against my neck. I could not breathe, I could not move. I began to struggle for release, but no avail. I opened my eyes and looked into the face of my husband.

His eyes shone like new money in the night, and his demeanor spelled trouble for me. The harder I wiggled the more, I was blocked. Using my hands, I began to hit against his massive arms, and nothing happened. Slowly I began to feel weak and tired. Without missing a beat, the nicotine on his breath captivated my nostrils as his voice said in a luring way, "I'm going to see if you really believe God." I was to the point of passing out as he released me. I motioned upward to catch my breath, but he grabbed me again before I could get away and this time he squeezed me harder, angrier. This time he let me go. I jumped up and William stood up. I became frantic as I saw him standing there. Frantically he blurted out, "Grace! What's wrong with you?"

Between tears and rattling nerves, I spoke with anger all over me, "You tried to strangle me! God,

147

William you tried to kill me. What have I done to make you do such a thing?"

William came closer to me, but I moved away since I was afraid. He stopped short and spoke with sadness, "I have done no such thing. You were squirming in bed, so I got up to get you a fresh cup of water. When I opened the door, you sat upright in the bed, staring at me with glossy eyes as if I were a stranger."

"William what is going on with me? I don't get it. I haven't had a feeling like this in a long time."

"Babe, I don't know. What did you dream?"

"It was not a dream! It was as real as you and I are sitting right here" I frantically spoke.

"Ok. I'm sorry. I mean what do you say happen?"

"I just left Sister Anna's room. You were sleep. I got in bed thinking. Before I could go to sleep, you were on me strangling me. You said I'm going to see if you believe God."

"What? Why would I say that? Why would I be strangling you in the first place?"

"I don't know the answers but yes, that is what you said to me. Not just that, but you had a devilish look in your eyes, and it made me think."

"Think what?"

"It made me think that something is going on and I need to get things together."

"Like what?"

Between the crying and feeling like a nervous wreck I could only say, "That is just that. I don't know, but all I know is what I saw and that was you strangling

149

me with that look in your eyes that I have never seen before."

"We know that whatever this is, Christ knows, and we must pray. We must rebuke this spirit of fear and auditory hallucinations off you right now."

How is it that I didn't think about that first? I know, I know better, and I know that I know that prayer is the first thing you do. Puzzled and uneasy, William anointed my head, and I raised my hands. This position isn't all that new to me, but to be on the receiving end is. I am usually the one that gives out the prayer, but this early morning I gladly accept the prayer. My spouse said, "Clear your mind of everything else and put your thoughts on Christ and what he has done for you. I don't have to tell you to repent of your sins, but to be in order. You must repent of your sins and ask for

God's forgiveness and thank HIM for your deliverance."

"I know. I am ready."

Without waiting anymore, he placed his hand on my head. As he began to pray as the spirit gave him utterance, "I speak to Grace's mind. All spirits of doubt, confusion, and fantasy, I break the chains you have linked up in her mind in the name of Jesus by the blood of the lamb. You foul spirit of mind control you no longer control the way she thinks, and her thoughts are not your thoughts according to the beginning of Proverbs twenty-three and seven says how you think, that is how it is. This day Jesus rules and reigns in her heart and soul, there is no room for passivity, all hedges are broken down and all tentacles are destroyed. You have no dominion over her, and you are cast down in the name of Jesus."

Immediately I felt the presence of the Lord all over me and to mind was the little boy that came to me after the service. As if I was thrown back in time. Plain as day, I remembered the things I had buried long ago. The tears flowed like a never-ending river. By way the tears poured down, I was crying out. My soul cried out for what I did not know. The Holy Spirit began to intercede as I opened my mouth and allowed the Christ in me to have HIS way. The more I would bend over the more the spirit of God would speak. These suppressed memories continued to come alive in me. The way the Holy Spirit showed me my past life, the more I cried out.

I had tried so hard to forget about what happened as a child the more I am faced with pain and demons. I dredge up old pain and things that no one knew I witnessed all those years ago. Now here I am a woman of great power in God, crying out for I had given birth to the demon that was for the New Era. That night seeing that child I delivered from my loins, that spirit, that sacrificial offering to Molech, in the flesh is now alive and for what and how when I saw them cut the child's veins? I continued to cry for I still could not believe how I could have placed in the back of my mind what happened to me.

The look the child had that day, many years passed and how I saw up close and personal the fruit I bore, made me weep more. I was more confused as my past invaded my present. For the life of me I didn't know why, but the Holy Spirit brought those things back to my remembrance. As clearly as if I were there, I my mind recollected every detail I hid, and every moment I spent in the compound. I could not quite recall the details, but there I was having the entire commemoration being played before me.

All in my heart, the word *secrets* kept coming forth. However, I have never told my husband of my past. I could not tell him what I did not remember. He had never known of the child I had or of its reason. William was clueless to my bygone life and so was I. With this truth, I cried and cried. I wept sorrowful, but breaking my time in my past was the voice of my husband saying, "That's it. Let it go don't stop until God let go of you."

It is at that instant that I opened my teary eyes and stared into his innocent face. How can I tell him that the demons are coming, and it is because of me? I had no idea how he would handle the bygone years. I must tell him; although, I dreaded it. With a question on his lips William spoke, "Babe, what is wrong? What did God reveal to you?"

I still did not speak. I continued to keep my hands uplifted, and my head perched toward heaven as I cried. Though, the more I went back in time the more in tuned I became. My tongues were extra as the awareness of my life came up-front in my memory. Numbness to the surrounding of my present, I wept for my past. My legs began to buckle as I stood there. William caught me as I was falling down. Using his massive arms, he led me to our bed. Easing me onto the plushy pillow top, I sat on the bed, and he sat beside me.

My head knew where it needed to be as it rested upon his shoulder and cried. Words would not form and I honestly don't believe I would allow them to either. Softly he spoke to my heart, "You can tell me."

I still did not respond to his statement. I weakly said, "I need to lie down."

My husband swiftly helped me back onto bed. I lay there, sobbing uncontrollably. I know William tried to figure out what was the matter with me, but this something I have to deal with. My love my not understand what I have been through and don't know if I would chance it. Be though as it may, I cried myself to sleep. This next morning, I awaken with a lot on my mind and a weary heart. I sat up in the bed and sighed heavily. With caution, I got out the bed and went to my skirt.

Being skeptic, I placed my hand in my pocket and brought out the locket. I already knew whose it was, but still not convinced. I opened the locket and gasped loudly. I heard William yell out, "You awake dear?"

In a flash, I hid the locket beneath my pillow and lay back down. William came in and said, "I thought I heard you up here."

"You did."

He walked closer to me and sat beside the bed and stroked my hair.

"You ok?"

"Yes, I am. That prayer you prayed was on time and I thank you."

"Grace, you don't have to thank me for doing what am I already called to do."

"I know, but the Spirit of God opened up many things to me because of it."

"If you want to tell me I am here for you and I will listen unbiased."

I could not answer him, and I would not answer him. Before I could tell him about my past, I must first

157

understand it; therefore, I spoke to change the subject, "How are our house guests doing this morning?"

"They all up and in good cheer, but I don't think they are leaving so soon because the house has to be repainted, and other precautions must be met because of the scare last night."

"I know they are welcome to stay here if Sister Anna wants too."

"I haven't addressed her about it because I do have joint custody, and I can't just leave her out in the cold."

"If she wants to stay she can. No problem."

William got up, and said, "You want some breakfast or not?"

"I am not hungry. I need to think."

"You still need to eat."

Smiling, I said as I sat on side the bed, "Thanks for seeing when I don't see."

"We are a help to one another and you coming into my life when you did actually saved me from making a mistake of following my flesh and not what the Spirit says."

It did not seem like my William to say things of such so I smiled, and spoke cheerfully, "I tell you what. I will have toast, orange juice, and a boiled egg. For fruit, a yellow apple."

He leaned into me and brushed his lips lightly against my lips. William gave me that smile that gave me a sense of comfort. "Breakfast will be ready momentarily so get dressed."

He left me alone with my thoughts and the locket. That time without wasting time, I opened it and saw my mom and dad's picture. I wanted to faint. I hadn't seen a physical picture of Mother Carol and Father James since I was a mere child. My hands began to shake as I dropped the locket onto the bed. I was trembling as I was speechless.

Regaining my composure, I picked the locket back up and wondered how did this child retrieve such a priceless heir loom of long ago? For the life of me, I could not grasp how it could be. Closing my eyes and squeezing the precious gift tightly, my mind rambled about the day Mother Carol gave it to me and how happier she appeared. That was the last time I had ever seen her so happy.

It was the night my mother and I had time together. It is also the time I was chosen by Majesty Leader. The very mention of his name to my mind caused my head to turn towards my shoulder as I smiled. How could that name make me blush like a schoolgirl? How was that name so connected to me that I couldn't remember? I personally thought and thought of the name and why I felt butterflies all over from the mention of it. A flash went off in my head. How could I have forgotten my Majesty Leader? How could I have forgotten our Majesty Leader? There was no way I should have placed him in the back of my mind and left him there. If I thought about anything I should have thought about him. But instead, when I closed my mind to my past, I closed all connections to it until then.

To reminiscence, it was the time I spent with him when I was eight. I thought about the candy, the hand games, tender smiles, and the wine. How could I have forgotten about the wine that made things more durable? How could I have forgotten the only man to have seen me naked? It has been three years and my own husband hasn't seen me naked. With a naïve smile,

161

I thought about how to a child his interactions were appropriate without the purpose. It is funny how I am actually thought back to a phase in my life when I was first exposed to the explosion of sex.

At first, I was scared like any other, but once I began to want Majesty Leader, the ugliness went away. In point of fact, I wanted him just as much as he was taking me. I panted after a man that was twelve years older my senior. It was something about the way he would look at me and how the intense conversations we would have as we talked before the sex. He made me at ease in his presence. It sounds silly to hear me think these thoughts, but I cannot escape the truth for Christ knows if I am lying and the last thing I need to do is to lie to myself.

Lying back onto my bed, I could see the way his hair bounced back and forth as he entered me. The way his eyes were closed as he took my virgin body only created moments for me to think back; however, he would clamp down his eyes before expelling himself into me. When he would do that, his fist squeezed the covers next to me. The scent of his breath, the scent of sex altogether, made me squirm in the bed for I summon up the penetration he did to me. It's not that my husband does not love me, but it is different.

I can't explain it, but it is just different. I want to assume I have harbored these sentimental thoughts because I was a young child with the leader of the compound, who found me worthy enough to take into his house and his bed. Using a deep sigh with my eyes closed, I could literally smell the scent of the room. In every area of the room, I could see him and I talking and playing hand games. At one point, I was in the mirror with him and he was telling me how filled out I was to be my age. He told me he thought I was beautiful and the beam on my face brightens any gloom sensation that I previously had.

I thought clearly, I recall going back to my parent's home, being dejected and lonely. The time I had with him was treasurable, especially in a girl's eye. I was the envy of all the girls, and I thought I had done something because I was handpicked by our leader to be a part of the New Era. Opening my eyes, I glared at the ceiling and thought how I have not allowed myself to feel or even think about anything or anyone that was before my grandparents. I did not want to conjure up memories that I depressed into my outer thoughts. I could not dare think about my brothers whom I didn't remember seeing or remember for that matter.

I just pretended that life never happened and for years it worked until then. I can answer everyone else's situations, but there I was with one of my own. To be honest, in some form, Majesty Leader had my heart, and I never got it back. I could only assume that was one of the reasons why I had never permitted another man to touch me. I could only continue to glare at the ceiling because it took over twenty-five years and a locket to figure out that I was still a child on the inside, who is in love with another man. I still couldn't believe that I never thought about my life or the man that helped changed my life.

I recognized that was why I was done in part and a prisoner to the compound in some form. My past life was why I still had dreams and why I did not want to bring up pain. The occurrence of that timespan also became why I was so bent on setting the captive free, but I was a victim of the very thing I see in people. I did witness my mother being overtaken by a demonic being and from time to time I hear her in my dreams. I have even glimpsed her, but my existence during this time is far away and not wanted to neither recall nor tell. This does not make up for anything, no matter how much I can preach the Word of God and no matter how I can prophesy. I had demons I must put to rest.

"Grace come on down" I heard William yell out.

Within myself, I thought I am not ready at all. I yelled back, "One minute."

I took the locket and put it among other jewelry as I went to take a quick shower. When I dried off and put regular house garments, I went downstairs. Upon reaching the base, the twins were in their highchairs and Sister Anna was in my usual seat feeding the children. I smiled for they were darlings.

"Sit here," William spoke as he pointed.

166

Taking the seat opposite to my husband, Sister Anna spoke with cheer as always, "Good morning."

"Good morning. How did you sleep?"

"I slept wonderful, thanks for asking."

"Sister Anna and the children will be here a little longer."

"That's fine. I want you all to be safe when you go home. Stay as long as you need too."

"Minister Grace, I don't want the babies and I to be a problem."

"You all are family and family help family, besides you are in the Lord and what better than to have a family member living right."

"Ladies, you have to excuse me. I have to get going today."

"Today is Saturday."

"I know we supposed to take the children to the park, but something has come up and I have to go to the office today. I'm sure the two of you can handle a set of babies."

I could not remind my husband, in front of company that this is his responsibility and he knows how I feel about being left alone with the children in general. He saw it in my face. William spoke, "I tell you what. I will meet you both at the park and we will have a fun day."

"You promise?"

"I do."

He walked over to his grand babies and gave them each a lovely peck, and then he kissed me on the cheek. Before walking out the door he spoke, "Sister Anna watch her, for me."

Sister Anna laughed heartedly as she spoke, "I sure will."

We all laughed as William left us alone. She finished feeding the children and went to change their clothing. I finished my breakfast and cleaned up the kitchen. Something did not right in the atmosphere. I have been off a little bit because of my own situation but I know when the Spirit has something to say. I have never been so engrossed like I am right now.

"You ready?"

I jerked back and it was Sister Anna.

"I scare you?"

Laughing, I stated, "Yes, I was lost in thought."

"Now that is a first. We are ready."

The children were dressed similarly as she had them in the buggy and her baby bags on her shoulder.

"You look like a natural."

169

"I don't feel like a natural."

I took the bags from her and she said, "Where is the park?"

"We are going to the one by William's job. It has nannies there to watch the children so the parents can get a break and it's about a mile from here."

"That sounds nice."

"That is why we are going to walk, and I will pay for the children to be watched while we watch as well."

I opened the door, and she walked out first; while, I locked the door.

"This way."

"You have a lovely house."

"Yes we do. Thank you."

"I mean it. You and William have chemistry, and you work so well together."

170

"Our chemistry is God and it's by HIS grace we work as the bible says."

"My husband, God bless his soul was a powerful man in God until the day he passed on. I miss him so much."

"I believe it."

"I get lonely and wish I had someone to talk to. I have been asking the Lord for a companion and so far I'm still alone."

She laughed to humor me, but I could feel the pain in her words.

"He will be on time when he comes."

"I hope he is as kind as your William is to you. It is rare these days to have a man find you and he is wonderful, all you could want in a man."

"You are so right. I like talking to you."

"I'm glad you do."

We walked longer without saying a word. We were relaxing as we took turns pushing the children. Before we made it to the park, she asked, "You two plan to have children?"

Taking my time to answer I spoke, "If that is in the Will of God, but as for now, the twins are ever so much all I could ask for."

Little Daniel began acting up. I knew they were ready to get down because I was just as tired of pushing. I paid for the nanny to watch them as we watch her. Sister Anna and I sat on the bench and began enjoying a snow cone.

"So, tell me new things about yourself."

"Well let's see. I am a widower with a pair of children I have to raise with the help of a kind man and woman."

I started laughing, and said, "Something else."

172

"I need a man. I'm lonely and I want to have sex."

"Whoa. Too much information." We laughed again.

"I'm serious. I haven't had sex in a while, and I am eager to get back at it."

"Be patient and I know you think I can say that because I have a man, but I say that for it is true."

If only she knew that my husband and I have not ever had sex. He was waiting on me, but I couldn't bring myself to sleep with him and to be honest, sex does not cross my mind like that. I had talked to him about it and he assured me that he was willing to wait for me. So far, he had. The time would come for us to finally have the encounter he waited so long on.

"Earth to Minister Grace."

"I'm back now" I spoke as we laughed. We began facing forward and watched the nanny as she played with the children. Suddenly something covered my eyes and kissed my neck.

"This better be my husband if not I have some serious explaining to do."

William removed his hands off me and sat next to us as he spoke to Sister Anna.

"Where are the children?"

"They are right there playing with the nanny."

"Oh no. We are to play with them and not that stranger."

"You know she is not a stranger."

"Babe, you know that I can't help it because of my profession in early childhood education. I mean we are to be the one's playing with them. Children learn by play and interaction."

"You are right, but I am not in the mood. I am tired."

"I will go play with them," Sister Anna spoke as she got up.

"Knock yourselves out. I will sit and watch."

William took off running toward his grand babies and Sister Anna walked in a trot behind him. I couldn't get into the whole grand parenting thing. I like seeing the children, but when it was time for them to leave, I was more than ready to see them off. The more I watch them the more they seem to have fun. I was picking up a vibe that she thinks we want custody, but she is badly misinformed. Unless Christ says so, I say no.

They all were enjoying themselves, and then I heard someone behind me demand, "Don't turn around and look at me."

Frigid was my movement as my ears became attentive to whoever it is. "Gracie, you are powerful, but you are weak. Turnaround from your present and face your past."

I made a twitching notion and when I turned around there was no one. William saw my facial expression and came over, "You ok? You look like you have seen a ghost."

"You didn't see anyone move from behind me?"

"No. You were there alone, and you had the look of confusion on your face."

Puzzling and confusion were all about me as I try to rationalize what just happened.

"Didn't you see someone talking to me?"

"No. You have been sitting here alone."

"William, someone was just here talking to me and they sounded real."

"Gracie, you okay? Ever since the other night you have been different."

"No! I am not crazy! Someone was just here talking to me."

"What did they say?"

I could tell that he disbelieved what I was saying so I played it off by stating and laughing, "You know I was probably daydreaming."

I wasn't sure if he believed it, but he spoke, "That's ok, we all daydream."

"Tonight, will I be able to be with my wife?"

The answer was no, and I didn't like giving him false hope. Before I could answer Sister Anna yelled out, "Everything alright?"

I waved as William spoke, "It's good here."

He gave me a light kiss and went back to playing with the children. To see my husband with

177

those children made me grin for he was happy. I mean literally happy. He was like a child himself, playing with them. I did not see Sister Anna walk up.

"Wishing you had children?"

Looking up I smiled, and spoke, "No, just watching them play before they realize we live in a cruel world."

She sat beside me and spoke, "You know, I think back to when William's son Daniel was alive. He loved my daughter with everything he had and William is alike him in many ways."

Placing my hand on hers, I spoke kindly, "If it hurts you to talk about it, you don't have to."

"I know, but it does the soul good to have it out and not bottled in."

"You're right."

"We all used to have dinners together as we anticipated the arrival of the twins, his wife and son with my family. Even after his wife past, William and I still tried to carry on, but it was not the same and before I knew it he was getting married to you."

"I understand this was all before me."

"It's just that one can't help, but to think about times of long ago before I lost my only child."

She took in a heavy sigh as she watched the children play with my husband. I asked, "Are the children like your daughter and his son?"

"I see my daughter in them every day, just as much as I see Daniel. They are the spitting image of our lost children, and it is through them, we are connected. The loss of a child can be traumatic, but William had been there all the way to make sure they are provided for."

"The children have the both of you as grandparents."

"They have you, too, Minister Grace."

"They have me on the spiritual sided and for guidance."

"Contributing something beats contributing nothing and spiritual is more important than the natural."

"Let us go to the stand and buy ice cream for them to enjoy."

We got up and I heard the Spirit say, "Secrets."

I stopped as I heard it as plain as day.

"What's wrong?" Sister Anna asked as she became puzzled for my sudden stop.

"I just heard the Lord say secrets."

"Secrets?"

"Yes secrets."

We stood for a few more minutes then I spoke, "Come on, lets go on to the stand."

Sister Anna and I got the ice cream and made our way over to an empty table. Seconds later William and the children came over. She wiped them off with wipes and gave them ice cream.

"You ladies are no fun."

"How so?" Sister Anna asked with humor and William replied back with humor, "You both are on the bench and not mingling, party poopers. If you are not playing talk to others here, who knows who you can win to Christ? But, the object is for you to come out and take a break. I'm sure the Lord doesn't want you to be all work and no play."

"Today honey, I am relaxing and you know I will do whatever the Lord tells of me."

"Minister Grace is right. I am relaxing and who knows what you learn."

William wiped the children off and took them back out to play. He was more energized than he was before. The children were having so much fun as he played with them. It is a sight I would not forget for my husband was happy and alive again. Sister Anna packed up the children's things, and I asked, "You need me to help?"

"No, I got it. I've been doing this motherly thing for a very long time and there is a certain way I pack their things. You know a woman puts her things a certain way and she expects it to remain that way, especially if she has her own children."

That kind, of made me look at her funny when she spoke, "This motherly thing and her own children." I know I am not a mother in the natural, but she could have said it better than that. Then again, she does have worldly ways and needs deliverance. Nicely I said, "Oh, I'm sorry you are right. What was I thinking, when a woman does things one way, she likes for them to be done that exact same way."

"That came out sour didn't it?"

"Yes it did. It came out very sour."

"I almost lost them and I don't want to lose them like I did my daughter and Daniel. He was like a son to me and I have taken on the responsibility of being their main primary care provider. I didn't mean any harm."

"It's fine. It has been a long day and you are just as tired as I am."

William brought the children over, and spoke, "I have to go back to the office. I will be home later. I'm going to do a short fasting today. The enemy tries us, but we must be strong and prevail."

"You want me to fast with you for a few hours?"

"No this is something I must do."

"Ok."

He kissed me good-bye and raked his hands through the children's hair as his way of saying later. Sister Anna and I loaded the children in their buggies and began to walk home. She talked and I didn't hear her. I was listening to the spirit in her. The long walk back home and watching my husband and Sister Anna play with the children tired me out. When we got back I did not eat, but washed off and went straight to bed. I laid there thinking, about the demeanor of Sister Anna. I picked up a vibe again she thought we wanted the children, but that was so far from true on my behalf.

When William got home, I would discuss it with him. I knew he would love it if they lived nearby, but I didn't know if I would like that. I'm not use to having them around, any children for that matter. My entire life has been uninterrupted and to have them there that weekend was too much already. I shook my head at the sheer thought of them lingering around longer. I hope her house is ready within a day or so. I am anxious to be returned to normal. Getting on my side, I stared out the window and spoke, "Lord, you use me to fix everyone, but me. I didn't know I was broken until now. Fix me, Lord. Fix me."

About twenty minutes later William came in the bedroom. I sat up on my elbows and spoke, "I am glad you are home. I need to talk to you."

He came over and kissed me on the forehead to say, "How things go after I went back to the office?"

"Odd at first, but it changed once we walked closer to home."

"How so?"

"Sister Anna thinks we want the children."

"Did she say that?"

"No, the spirit in her says that."

"Oh, but if I want more time with them, she has to obey or be prepared for a battle."

"I'm sure it can be settled out of court, if it leads to that. You and her are the only living close relatives those children have."

"I'm just saying because I have felt that spirit of denial and thought it was nothing to be worried about."

"Any spirit you feel, is something to be worried about. It is when it is small you must be on your best guards. It is the little things we must be concern about. Everything starts minor before it turns big."

"My grandmother use to say a stitch in time saves nine."

"Yeah, that sounds about the same thing."

William continued to undress as he asked, "What all you say happened again?"

I got out the bed and said, "I asked her if she wanted me to help her and she said something about having own children and how she's been doing this motherly thing for a long time and there is a certain way she pack their things."

"Motherly things?"

"Yes, motherly things, and then she apologized for the way it sounded when it came out her mouth."

"She probably feels threaten by you."

"How?"

"We are married, and we have a more stable home for the children."

187

"That does not mean we want the children here all the time."

William faced me to say with a strong thought, "What if I do? What if I want to them here more?"

"William, I don't know. Is this something you have been thinking about?"

"No, I haven't been thinking about it, but it would be nice to have the children here more often. I never dreamed that I would miss them until now. I would like to be more involved in their lives while they are young, do you understand?"

"I love you and if that is what you want lets seek God before we make mistakes."

"You are right, and I pray this is what HE wants for it is the desire of my heart to be closer to the only blood of my son."

"You think she would move closer to us?"

"Nah I don't think she would consider it because she is faithful to her church. You know also that you both went through something like this when your children first passed away."

"My understanding is parents do what is in the best interest of the child and not for themselves. They no longer have a life and if moving closer to us would be more beneficial for the children, then she should not hesitate to come."

"I agree, but moving takes a lot of things and for her to uproot all she has known to come here would be awkward for her."

"William how is it awkward if we offer to pay for her to have a place to stay and in return all she has to do is live close by?"

"We can talk to her about it."

"No, you can. I can sit there and not voice my opinion because to her I am just a step grandparent and not blood relation like you both are. To keep the enemy out of it, I will sit by, but if I feel like something is not right, I will shout it out."

"Tomorrow I will make plans to talk to her about it."

We got in bed, and both just laid there unmoving and full of thoughts.

"Today as I was walking to the ice cream stand, I heard from the Lord. HE said secrets."

"What does that mean?"

"I don't know, but I know HE will reveal them if there be any."

"Grace, I'm confident that we are on the right track and the enemy will try and show his head somewhere. If he doesn't then he is not doing his job

190

and we both know he is going to do his job. We just have to do ours."

Out from nowhere I spoke, "I am not the motherly type."

He cut me off to say, "Don't say that! That is what the enemy would try to use to hold over your head, but he won't do it. Not on my watch. Grace, you can be just as much a mother than any woman. You have based your entire life around the things of God and now this marriage. I know we haven't made love, but I am patient enough to wait until you are ready. Don't fall prey to the enemy that lurks in dark places of our mind. He will use all kinds of tactics just to get us out of a place with God."

"I can always tell you what I think and you know how to make it right. That means much to me. I just had an experience that transformed me more than I knew. I desire so much to consummate our marriage, but I just can't and I don't know when. What I do know, is it will be on time."

"God brought some things back to you the other day, didn't HE?"

"Yes."

"You want to talk about it?"

I don't even know how to deal with this new information, let alone talk about it. I have to first figure for myself what is going on. I thought carefully then spoke, "Not now. I have a speaking engagement across town on next Wednesday. You plan to come?"

"No, you and Sister Anna can go and I can watch the children."

"What if she doesn't want to go?"

"To not give place to the devil, I will go."

"William, I trust you and if you don't want to go, you don't have to."

"I know you do, but that is not the problem."

"Well, what is?"

"I can't explain it."

"I know what you mean."

"Grace, I want to make love to you, but you won't let me. I am a man that wishes to have you."

"William, I know that and sex, money and lack of communication are the main things people divorce but we are not those people. We have the Lord with us and in us."

I can tell that he is deep in thought as he lay next to me. I closed my eyes, and he said, "At least seek God about it. I can only be strong until my flesh gets weak, then what?"

"We pray it doesn't get to that, William."

As I turned over, I spoke softly, "Goodnight."

It is not that he does not do anything to me, but I had I given my heart and body away years ago to another man and I haven't gotten it back. Since the new discovery, I tried to understand how I could not want my husband. I use to think it was because I was so wrapped up in the things of God that I never had time for relationships. Truth of the matter was I only wanted a relationship with Christ. Giving my-self to Christ and delivering people had been my only mission.

Getting married and becoming a grandparent were not a part of my life. However, I acquired those things when I married William and to know he would soon want us to have a baby once we made love. Turning to face him, I thought how he was what the world called every woman's dream and I had it all. From a worldly aspect, my husband was the type of man you wanted. His tight upper body cavity begs to hold you and his soft smile melts away anything you need, but yet I did not want his loving.

I haven't been able to come to terms with sex since I was young. I thought back to the night we attempted it, but I got sick and dreaded it. The Word told us in First Corinthians Chapter seven Verses three through five talks about what is the wife is the husband and vice versa. How no matter how you may not want to give your husband or wife your body, it is not yours to hold onto. It also talked about to only be away from your spouse for a period of praying and fasting. If you don't get back together, the enemy will come in tempt you away from your spouse. Before I closed my eyes, William said, "I am tired of you teasing me and pretending to be traumatized. You are going to give me what I am rightfully entitled to."

"What?"

Using his weight, William straddled me and placed his power arm under my neck. This was new to me as my husband held me down. I tried to look into his eyes, but they were solid white. He appeared to be possessed and I began praying. He howled at me then spoke, "Pray again and I will break your neck!"

I was afraid all over again then the pain. It wasn't like the pain I experienced with Majesty Leader, but more hurtful. William was inside me and taking me like a mad man. I could only think of a happy place and that happy place was with Majesty Leader. Soon as he came, he got off me and went to sleep. Here I am hurt, astounded, older, but in mental pain. How could my husband have raped me? How could he take what could have been a great moment and flipped it? My thoughts were all over the place as I wept.

The morning came, but not fast enough for I was still curled up in a ball, sitting in the recliner. I could see his hand fishing for me on my side of the bed. When he saw that I was not there he sat up, wiped his eyes and spoke when he saw me, "Babe you ok?"

I continued to sit and rock for I was still not sure of what all happened. I had been sitting here all night and still dazed. Through all my turmoil, I was sure of one thing and that was, he raped me.

"Grace, you ok? Babe talk to me" he spoke as he got up and came toward me.

In a low tone that could barely be heard I stated, "You raped me."

William stopped. He had a worried look upon his features as he said with doubt, "Raped you?"

"Yes you forced yourself on me. You held me down and entered me without permission."

"No, I didn't do anything like that. I couldn't have."

Standing to my feet, I became stern when I said, "How are you going to tell me that you did not rape me when I was wide awake? You were possessed by an evil spirit as you pinned me down and took our precious moment away."

I turned my back on him and allowed the tears to fall silently as I sat back in my chair rocking. He did not look at me when he said quietly, "I thought it was a dream, and we were role playing. I had no idea that it really happened. I can't believe that I actually raped you."

Without placing my eyes on him I spoke, "You told me that you are tired of me teasing you and it's time for you to take what is rightfully yours."

My husband came closer to me and got on his knees in front of me. I did not budge. I continued to hold my knees in my arms as he sat on the floor.

"I am sorry for doing this to you. I had no idea. To me we were role playing and I could not believe that you changed your mind and decided to let me make love to you."

"You were possessed for a moment. The enemy is using your inner thoughts and sleep to come at me. The thing is, when I looked in your face, I knew you were not you. I knew it was not the man I married taking me."

"Do you remember any of it?" I asked, needing to know.

"I remember we talked for a few moments then I heard you tell me that you were ready and you want to give it a try. I did not act at first because I thought you might be sleepy then you said take me like a mad man, you want to role play. I did, but I don't remember physically doing it. I thought I brushed it off and went on to sleep."

"I can tell you; you entered me. Look at the blood in the bed."

William got up and went towards the bed and there was blood. He spoke, "You sure it is not your menstrual?"

"Yes! I am sure!"

We both continued not speaking, but thinking. He then said, "Maybe it is best if I move into the other room. I don't want to be in the room with you in case the enemy catches me weak again or anything."

"Our line with God must have a breech for things like this to come up."

"I am still sorry, Grace, so sorry. I would never do anything to hurt you, not ever."

"It is ok because I know the enemy is in our home, spiritually."

"You right. We will tell Sister Ann that you are fasting and not to be bothered."

"I will be fasting for the next three days, and this would be a great opportunity for you to be downstairs, enjoying your grand babies."

William got up to get some of his clothes out of the room. I sat there, lost in thought and unemotional. I could tell that my husband was bothered like I was, but he did not fully understand the enemy. He never seen it take a love one and transform. He tried to find the good, but you can't find what is not there in the enemy. The next three days were peaceful. I prayed and studied God's Word. I fail to recall my memories because they

201

were not widespread in my mind. I had placed what I went through on the back and continued to listen to the spirit as HE spoke to me. Nothing mattered to me, but closing the breech that may be contaminate. I was without a doubt knew that the enemy was after me and my husband.

I refuse to wait around while the enemy lied in wait for us to dissipate. We were stronger together and soon enough I would overcome my own demons and be the wife he needs me to be. I opened the windows, and the fresh cool air entered the room. Quickly, I showered and got dressed. I didn't know if anyone was in the house for it was quiet. The children, I would hear every so often, but not enough to count. Even Sister Anna was singing. That's a first, I thought as I came out of the three day fast and prayer.

Making my way downstairs, I saw a note that William had left.

It read: Miss you bunch and can't wait to see you. I have taken everyone to the church as we wait for your awesome message from God. Love William.

That gave me so much hope that my husband was on the right track as myself. I feel that he and Sister Anna overcome any differences they might have had about the children. I felt better about that night as I grabbed an apple and a bottle of water.

I was greeted by a nice lady as I opened the doors of The Christian Faith Walk Missionary Baptist Church Sanctuary. The choir sung *Walk with me Lord*, the old fashion way. The room was bright and scent of fresh flowers could be smelled. The floor was of a thick dark blue carpet material. The benches were dark purple with flowers on the end of each row and at the end were Ushers dressed in all white. Each woman had one hand behind her back and the other one to the side.

To the right of me was the Mother board section and the Deacon board was to the left. I walked through the choir stand isle, which is right behind the pulpit to the side podium. Out the corner of my eye I thought I saw my mother. I looked again and it was not her. No one was there. Shaking off the notion, I made it to the podium. Clearing my head, I kneeled and thanked Christ for HIS strength and HIS Word. Getting up, I sat at the seat.

The lady that greeted me called my name and the people clapped. I watched the people and how few there were. It mattered not because I know who all is here, are all predestined to be here. Standing in front of the visitor's podium, I got up with my bible and placed it upon the stand. Observing the crowd, I spoke out loud, "Let us pray. Gracious God above any God, decrease me and increase YOU for the people. I myself can't do anything without you; therefore, I speak, as I believe you have given me utterance. Close their natural minds and open their spiritual minds so they may hear what thus saith the Lord and it is in your name Jesus alone, I pray Amen and Amen." Holding my head up, I observed the crowd again. This time with more authority, I spoke, "Everyone in the sound of my voice repeat after me. Lord, I confess with my mouth and believe in my heart that you gave up the ghost for me and you first love me. I repent this day of my sins all known and unknown. I ask that you cleanse me and sanctify me to be used at Your Will. I thank you for your grace and mercy. I thank you Lord and starting right now, I believe I am saved, and it is in your name Jesus, Amen."

Everyone said Amen as I stated, "I had prayed on another topic, but moments before I could make it to the doors, the Lord stopped me and told me something else. In fact, I will speak on you must be born again. If you have your bible please turn to Acts Chapter two, Verse four. This scripture talks about everyone there were filled with God's Spirit, the Holy Ghost. Not just that but they all spoke in tongue when the Spirit filled them. Everyone say Amen." The people repeated Amen. I again scanned the crowd and there I saw it. Giving a slight smile, I yelled loud as I could, "Happy birthday!" They all looked at me and the children grinned. With the microphone on my head I began to walk through the congregation. This is unorthodox and to them I am crossing the line, but that mattered not to me, it's the Christ in me. I stopped at a child and asked, "When is your birthday?"

"July twenty-eight."

I walked off from the child, and stated, "July twenty-eight is the day that child was born, but you are not truly alive until you have your birthday in Christ. I see some of you are confused. Once God's Spirit lives in you that is called the Holy Ghost, and it is that day you have a spiritual birthday. That day is the only day that made you a part of Christ. You will no longer be a stepchild but his child. You will have heavenly rights and you can't be an heir to the throne if you have not HIS spirit. " I walked off a few paces to allow what I just said to sink in. With more authority, I spoke, "When you lose our earthly ways you can find our spiritual ways. As long as you are in the flesh you can't comprehend things that are spiritual. You have to have Christ in the Spirit for those that worship HIM must worship HIM in Spirit and in truth. As long as you are in the flesh you will walk after the flesh. You will desire the things of the flesh. I know we are fleshly, but we must also learn how to be spiritual. You don't want to spend all your life just doing good deeds and never experience all Jesus has for you. For good deeds are just that good deeds. The Word says Old things are passed away and all things become new and the new you is the one that is born again." I made my way back to the side podium and said, "Turn to John Chapter three Verses one through seven. Think on this term, with your natural mind, you would think as Nicodemus did because being born of a woman is the only birth, but I am here to let you in on a well-known fact. Your natural birth comes from man, your spiritual birth is a gift from God who gives it freely to all that seek HIM and HE is the only one that can give you, HIS spirit. Why is having God's Spirit in you so important? It is the same importance as your biological child having a part of you in them. If a child does not have a part of you then that is not your child. You can dress it up all day long in other words pretend you live for God and at the end of the day when things are said and done, if the child does not have a part of you, it still is not your child. In other words, if you don't have God's Holy Spirit living, breathing, and operating in you, then you are still not HIS child. You can say what you want, if HIS Spirit isn't in you, it isn't in you."

The people were shouting so, that I thought I was in the wrong church. From the looks of the crowd, book sense people were still sitting. Therefore, I spoke, "You get twenty-three chromosomes from each parent and through the blood that is how specialist knows who your parents are. Once Christ cleanses you with HIS blood and HIS spirit manifests in you, then you are HIS child. Let me explain it this way, you have a child, and your sister has a child, is her child yours? No the child is kin to you and that is it, just kin. In God, you must be HIS child in order to be HIS. How can you be a child of God? Again by having HIS Spirit and what is HIS Spirit? The Holy Ghost or Holy Spirit, either one you prefer saying; however, this Godly Spirit must live inside of you. Just because you are kin to God, it does not make you a legal heir of God."

I paused and waited for the people to settle down. On the other hand, I saw this one man. He never moved or did anything, and the Spirit of God told me that I am going to deal with him, but not now. Seeing the stranger, I went on to speak, "Once you become a true child of God, Satan is no longer your father because you have your real father, which is Jesus Christ. John four and twenty-four says how God is like the wind, you can't see HIM, but HE is there. How can you worship HIM with something you don't have? Even if you have the true Word of God and not HIS Spirit, you still done in part. You are not whole. In Isaiah fifty-nine and nineteen middle ways of that Verse the Word of God says, when the enemy against you, the Spirit of the Lord, which is the Holy Spirit will stand up for you and fight. It will speak when you can't speak and it knows what to pray when you don't. You need the Spirit, it will lead and guide you, but you have to have the Spirit. There is no other way."

The people said Amen.

I heard the Spirit, and I spoke what it said, "Many of you are found in at the end of Mark Chapter seven Verse six. Some of you are doing lip service and not seeking God earnestly. Even the devil knows the word. You say all day, how much you love the Lord, but your actions speak louder than your words will ever say. It is good if it is in your heart to do what is righteous or what is commanded of thee, but it's not good enough for we are called to live holy. Good is just one aspect of doing what is right." The place began to settle down. I began walking down the aisle, saying, "Almost everyone has fallen into the condemnation of I am a child of God. They think because HE made them that they belong to HIM. The truth is HE made everything, but everyone does not know HIM. Many do not know who their spiritual father is. Jesus loves you, but HE loves those that do HIS Will even more. Just because HE made you does not mean you are HIS. A long time ago, my grandfather told me that a woman can have a child, and the child won't be hers. I thought he was foolish. To make a long story short, it took me a long time to get it. A woman can have a child and that is her child by law. But, if the child does not show its biological mother love that is not her child. I see some of you are lost. Let me say this, just because God created you doesn't mean you love HIM like HE would love you. The one you show your love to is the one you love. If you show more interest in worldly things, than the God of this world is your father. If you show more interest in spiritual things, than Jesus Christ can be your heavenly father once you have HIS spirit. You will cleave to one and reject the other. You cannot walk with God and be involved with the devil, God's arch enemy."

"Does your husband forgive, can you forgive?" My eyes went straightway to the evil spirit that was sitting near the back. Everyone gasped and started turning back to see who the accusation came from. I already knew that the enemy was there and who it would use. With the authority of Jesus Christ, I spoke, "I command you to tell me who you are in the name of Jesus!"

The spirit sat on the bench and stared at me. We did not do full eye contact as I picked up the oil. I spoke with caution and without hesitation, "Take the children and the unsaved out."

I know that demon spirits can enter through the eyes and worldly people like to watch things. They will not think to close their eyes and plead the blood of Jesus is against you Satan as demon spirits speak. I know that if they do not leave the room, more of them will need deliverance and these people aren't strong enough for such a work.

Giving the nod, I had my husband to leave with Sister Anna and the twins. William was a Godly man, but the area of deliverance was not his field. My husband could apply the Word to every situation, but he didn't know the name of evil spirits. He didn't live, breathe, and study how to use God's Word to fight the evil spirits that plague the people. He knows that I know what I am doing and how well the Lord uses me in this area. If I tell him to leave, he knows it is serious.

Everyone began leaving the room with only a few of us remaining. Those that remained oiled their eyes and forehead. Honestly, they all gave me the impression of being nervous and afraid. In good conscience, I didn't believe they had ever encountered anything like that and for the most they don't know what to expect. They also had sheets ready for covering and napkins and bucket for the purging. I spoke from the pulpit, "REVEAL YOURSELF, RIGHT NOW IN THE NAME OF JESUS BY THE BLOOD OF THE LAMB!"

The evil spirit knew the Lord was with me for it kept its head down and squirming as it spoke, "I am Resentment. I am Hatred. I am Violence and I am Murder. You torture me!"

I placed holy oil on the man, and he was hot to touch. In fact, it burned my hand some. That made me evoke a previous dream of years gone by, but I continued on, "I command you evil spirits linked to bitterness, unchain, unhook, and come out in the name of Jesus!"

"Never! This is my house. I live here."

Demon spirits refer to a person's body as their house and if they have been living in that person for a long time, they are hard to leave. The strongman is the demon spirit that has been there the longest and it will send smaller spirits out first before it comes out. If the person wanted to be help it must renounce the spirits that live in them. Once that was done the evil spirit had no right or legal ground to the person. I began to speak to the person, "Sir, do you believe Jesus died on the cross for you?"

"No, he doesn't!" the evil spirit spoke as it wiggled more.

The person on the inside softly spoke, "Yes, Jesus died for me."

"No! Never!" the evil spirit yelled out.

"You cannot live in the house of God and according to Matthew Chapter four Verses ten and eleven, we are to worship our Lord Jesus. Jesus is our God. When you worship Christ, you will let him be your Master once this is done the Devil left the person."

"NO! I CAN'T LEAVE THIS HOUSE. THIS IS MY HOUSE! YOU ARE TRESPASSING!"

"Say Satan, you are no longer welcomed in my house. Jesus Christ is my Lord, and I will serve HIM."

The man repeated it and he began to buck, holler, and spit everywhere. From that angle, I could tell that the spirits had been a part of his life, and the demon spirits did not want to let go. In all honesty, they never want to peacefully leave a body. They could do great damage if they are living inside a person. Everyone formed a circle around the evil spirit, while it sat in low posture. I stood in the aisle as I questioned the enemy by saying, "Look at me, in the name of Jesus."

The evil spirit made motions, and it brought back memories of the way my mother moved at the church. I hadn't seen anything like it until tonight. It quickly got me to thinking about the time Mother Carol and I were at a church similar to the one I just left. I made a quiver, and the evil spirit felt it. For spirits know when fear is upon you because that is how they keep people down. It looked up at me to speak slyly and slowly the same way my mother did, "Preacher, preacher, preacher, what's wrong preacher? You saw something you recognize?"

There within my mind, I began to call on the Lord for help. I needed him to help me, now more than ever. I needed the Lord to help me come up against the enemy that was using this man. Instantly I became restored as I spoke, "James Chapter four Verse seven states. "If you willingly give yourself to Jesus the Devil has to leave you. He can't be with you as long as you are with God. I command you by the authority of Jesus Christ of Nazareth to lose this body and go back to the pits of Hell.""

The person body started in spasm state. His arms were striving to reach up as to praise God, but the evil spirit fought mightily to keep the hands down. The man's legs were moving violently as they kicked the pews in front of him, while, his head winged back and forth numerously. The scene had the appearance of a body fighting to live. Some of the deliverance workers were petrified at the sight. The ones that were not, kept their eyes closed as they in low speech pleaded the blood of Jesus.

Loudly as possible I helped in by saying, "The blood of Jesus is against you Satan. You have no more legal right to that body you call house. You are trespassing on God's property! You are commanded in the name of Jesus Christ lose that body now!"

The man was hitting at his chest as if to bust it open. Each sound could be heard loudly as the fists came into contact to his flesh. The more he pounded away at his torso the more he would scream by making unknown sounds. He even sprung up and down as if he was leaping. The onlookers appeared to be surprised at the man's deliverance actions.

Suddenly, he began to purge up white, black, and green phlegm all over the floor, but some got into the small pails, the helpers had placed.

His eyes were bucked as his body became limp on the pew. Lights flickered as doors on the church flew open, and then shut. No one knew what to do. From the looks of it, the church deliverance teams needs more improvement. If I hadn't been there, the devil in that man may have made them all doubt the Christ in them. We all prayed to close the deliverance and I spoke before departing, "Don't touch him. Let the Lord continue to work on him as he is slain. When he wakes up, have a male mentor assigned to him. Let the person be someone in good standing with the church and a true a man of God. This person is to talk to the man about what occurred here tonight when they are strong enough to understand, discuss his salvation and importantly what Jesus did at the Cross on Calvary. Their sole purpose is to teach him about Christ and not give him leaven. If they teach him anything else, his next deliverance won't go so easy and believe me, it was easy. Once a person was delivered and they returned to whatever it is, they would be harder to deliver because the demonic spirit won't let up so lightly. They detest living outside of the human body."

The all stood there and stared at me as I spoke of the demonic spirit. From where I stood, they all are going to encounter more spirits and some far worse than what they experienced tonight. I went for my bible, left out the building and went home. That night's release of the evil filled man did not put me to ease, as it normally did. When an individual was liberated it pleases me deep down, but that feel was not found. The Holy Spirit in me was disturbed in some form. It was more like a warning about something is on the way; therefore, I began to pray in the Spirit.

After the Holy Spirit interceded, I was better not perfect just better. The whole trip I drove home, my mind kept thinking about the man Christ used me to deliver. He sat there the total service without moving, not even blinking. He continued to stare, as my mother did all those years ago at the man that was preaching. I could not tell what went on with him, just like I did my mother. He had the presence of someone screaming help me, just like my mother did.

So many things came from my past and it all started from the locket. All of those things happened over thirty something years ago and I was in my prime, there was my past. My mind gave thought to my favorite saying, 'I will understand in time.' Instantly, that line reminded me when I was talking to my grandparents. I asked about my mother's fate. Before they could answer I spoke, it did not matter I would understand in time.

However, I do not understand as I should. The evil filled man saw my fear and that has never happened in all my days of freeing captive people. Something so small, yet became big to me and the enemy saw it and almost fed off it. Shuttering at that thought, I continued driving. Then, my mind went back to the man at the service. His face was fixed while he glared at me. No one came to his aide because no one paid attention to him, just like they did my mother. It did not cross my mind until tonight just how someone really acts when they await deliverance.

Everything I have learned about spiritual warfare is being turned upside down and challenge. I don't even know why I waited so long to come to his rescue. It was like a part of me wanted him to go away, but the God in me would not have it. Lately my life had been tested by the very thing I tell people. All the more my past life came to life, I have a sense of doubt and that was unlike me. I drove more as I deliberated as my mind wondered back to the man. He was not into the service. It was like he was waiting on someone to notice so he stood out. In my ears, I kept hearing that hissing sound. Chills ran up and down my spine as I heard that sound again in my head. It brought back the time in my past, when I last saw my mother as my mother.

Suddenly in my vision was my mother and my thoughts went haywire. The eyes on my face grew about ten inches because I could not believe it. She had on the traditional dark blue dress with the white apron and bonnet to match. That was how she looked when I last saw her but the closer I got, she threw up her arms as to shield herself. I hit brakes and the car began to slide as I tried not to hit her, but it was too late. I hit her and when my front seat got to the point where she stood, Mother Carol sat in my car. I in haste, I hit the gas and kept my head straight. Everything about me became a wreck as I chanted over and over, "You're not real, you're not real. You're false evidence appearing real, a false evidence appearing real. This is a trick of the enemy, straight out of Hell and I rebuke it right now, in the name of Jesus."

"Oh my, Gracie, you are a true woman of God."

"I have really lost it. I can't believe my mother is in my car."

"But, I am. I am here."

"I've actually lost my marbles. I am in a car talking to a dead woman. This must be a dream. This has to be a dream."

"This is not a dream. I am in this car and I have to tell you a few things. I can assure you that I am real. I see you have the locket, but I am here to warn you as a mother warn her child."

"You are not real and I don't receive any accusations you have to say."

"Daughter, don't you want to know what happened that night at the church? That night that you were the only one left alive."

She had my attention. All my life I wanted to know all I could, but I was so young. No one was alive to tell me of the things that transpired, but me. Now here in my car was my mother and she wants to tell of the things I longed to hear. I don't even know if I should receive such words from a dead woman, but I was not thinking right and confused. I did not look for reasons of what I may see. I didn't feel ready and I wasn't sure of anything earthly anymore. Softly the melody of her tone flooded me with the spirit of persuasion.

Just her presence alone, took me back to years when I was a child. The idea of just being able to hear her speak allocated anything I was thinking. My ears became inclined to the voice I longed to hear. She said, "Clear your mind and listen. I ran from my parent's home because I met your Father James. He pretended to be Christian just to attract a chosen vessel and I was it. I was chosen to produce the New Era child, but didn't for the child was to be a boy, and then a girl. I was young and hopelessly in love, naïve you can say. I sold my soul to the devil just to have a given child for the man I loved. My ten sons were produced and when you were born I changed my mind. The devil came for me, but when he saw that I was pregnant with you, he decided that he wanted you, instead. I vowed not to let him have you and I would do all I can to stop him. I became more stubborn than ever to teach you Jesus, in hopes that you would save us. When you gave birth I realized that his spirit in me was too strong, that containing it would be a hard job. Time got away and you were too late. You

229

couldn't help you because you were young and you couldn't help me because you didn't know how. Satan's spirit had taken toll and it was stronger than my free will. I dared not look at you for I didn't know what the evil one had planned, so I ignored you. He had prepared a plan for me to kill you in the woods, but I wouldn't. The night I transformed into my true inner self, I tore the side of the building off to leave. My inner self fought with my outer self because I would not take your life like I did all the others. I had already given my parents precise briefings to be there when you come out the woods. I knew it was not going to make it but I prayed you made it."

I was quiet and don't know how I was driving and not speaking. Honestly, something would not allow me to speak but to listen. So, I kept listening in hopes she is telling me the truth.

"Before burying your past, you have wondered why you?" I did not respond because I didn't know anymore. My judgment was cloudy, and my thoughts are unstable as I drove faster towards home, my safety. " Let me tell you why you. I was to only have two children a boy and a girl, but after my first-born son, the boys kept coming. In this ministry, they believed all the wrong things. I have tried to take you away before the promise could be fulfilled, but that would mean killing us both. You would do more damage to the devil alive so I let that thought go. The thing is my first born was to mate with my last born, so the evil bloodline would be rich with sin." Mother Carol paused as if she was waiting on me to say something. I didn't. She next said, "The Majesty Leader you fell in love with is my first born and you are my last born. He is your oldest brother."

Within myself I said, what, what, my brother, my brother? After all the questions I asked myself, my mind replayed what my mother said again. I began to verbally yell no as I swerved and fought the steering wheel for control. In that instant I did not care if I lived of died. My entire life had been closed off from me because of the way I lost my mother. I had refused to think back on anything that happened before I turned eleven. To me I did not have a childhood. I only concentrated on the time I met my grandparents until the present. I didn't even think about my parents or the brother's I had never seen. All this was irrelevant to me and deemed unimportant.

I could not stop the tears. I would use one hand to wipe them away as I sniffled. How could I have known that Majesty Leader was my oldest brother? How could I have fallen madly in love at the age of eight? How could I not allow another man to get close to me because of the experience of sex and love? I had no idea. I had no clue. My mind was running a thousand miles as my thoughts raced frantically. The more I thought about it the more I fought for the tears to stop.

Suddenly, bright lights blinded me as I was wiping my eyes. I began to fight the steering wheel because I had lost control of my car. From nowhere, my body had the feeling of being tossed to and from by something strong. I must have driven off the road and the car was shaking me as it endured the rough path. On the left side of me, I heard William say, "Wake up, Grace! Wake up!"

Wait, William is not in the car with me, I thought. The rough shaking path had come short. I stopped screaming and fighting to slowly open my eyes to search all around me hysterically. I only found my husband's hands on me. My heart was thumping wildly as my breathing as my husband's face was paranoid. I did not know what to think. Looking downward, I glanced at my hands and noticed that I was in my bed. Instead of a steering wheel, I tussled with the sheet covers. A whimpering sound escaped my mouth as I jumped out the bed and fell to my knees crying. William got out the bed and came to me. He kneeled in front of me and placed his hands about my shoulders to around with tears in his voice, "You okay? Please baby talk to me. What is going on with you? I can't take what you are going through."

Still in a state of shock and unbelief, I did not answer him. Words would not form in my mouth. Truth of the matter is I didn't want to speak. He pulled me deep into his chest area and allowed me to cry like a baby. For the first time in a long time, I felt love. The love a man should feel for a woman. The more he held me the more I cried. Eros love is the type of love that husband and wives shared, but how was I to deal with the fact that I harbored Eros love for my brother and not my husband?

My stomach felt weak, and the few contents of my stomach did not remain, I began to throw up. William ushered me to the bathroom so I can place myself over the toilet to vomit. I assumed he went to clean up the mess because he left me alone. Moments later he came back in to check on me. I was empty from all the gagging I did. My husband helped me up and wiped my face with a cool towel. That helped some. Next he took off my night shirt and gave me a headache pill for resting.

I swallowed the pill and the water before he assisted me back into the bed. For a long time, sleep kept skipping by me. William continued to stare at me for he doesn't understand what is going on. The fact is, I don't think he will understand and I don't believe I can explain it. Something happened to me and I didn't know what went on, but whatever it was, I must face it head on. Later on I awoke and felt better than I did previously. I saw that it was late in the evening. Yarning, I washed up, and put on loose clothing. When I made it downstairs, the twins were at the table.

Sister Anna came out of the kitchen with her arms cups in each hand. The minute she saw me, her facial expression kind of dropped. She might be shocked to see me out the room and headed to the kitchen.

"Hey there, Minister Grace, how you been?"

Returning a happy smile, I replied, "I'm great, nice to see you as well."

She walked by me and spoke, "Sit down and have some supper, I made enough for everyone."

"Thanks. Where is William?"

"He is still at the office. He should be back in a few. He gave strict instructions not to disturb you because you had a long night last night, at church."

"Yeah, I did."

I prayed over the salad, spaghetti, and garlic bread she had placed before me. As she began to eat, she asked, "Would you like some wine?"

"No thank you. I don't drink, not even on special occasions as some do."

Sister Anna poured herself a tall glass of white wine and stirred it for a few moments. She closed her eyes before taking a sip. Soon as she removed the glass from her lips, she opened her eyes, and spoke candidly, "I don't even have to tell you, you know it's not a sin to drink. It's a sin to get drunk."

I slowly stopped chewing my food. I wiped my mouth with the napkin to say, "Romans fourteen and twenty-one says: It is not good to do things in front of someone if it will make them be halted in God, weak or offended in some form. That statement is true Sister Anna, but people drink to get drunk and if I could get drunk, stumble or be weak because of the drinking and I know that getting drunk is a sin, why would I want to drink?"

She began shaking her head to agree to my statement. She took another sip of the wine and responded, "Good point, but that is you. After taking care of two small ones and the day was hectic, you would need a drink. You may not have a hectic day or even tend to little ones as I do, but trust me you would

need a little bit every once and a while, just to relax and

ease your mind."

I continued to eat as she drunk her wine in

silence. Her character was different as I observed her. I

hadn't been near her in a while. It could've been just

me. The twins had finished. Sister Anna took them

down the hall to wash up and put them to bed. I

finished eating supper and had cut myself a huge slice

of lemon box pie. Before I could place my fork in it,

she came back in, and spoke, "I hope me drinking and

being in your home hadn't been a problem?"

"You have not been a problem and I'm sure

William is glad the children are here longer. As for the

drinking I would rather you didn't, especially around

the children."

She sat down at the table and cut herself a slice of pie. She did not respond. She glared at me with evil looking eyes. I stated nicely, "I have not been sociable to you as I would have been and it's not because I am not use to company. Between the studying, praying, fasting, and my own life, I have been having some kind of time, and it is unbelievable. Please forgive me?"

She lifted up her glass to say, "What is there to be forgiven for?"

Sister Anna sipped her wine as she rolled her eyes to say, "I'm in your home and as for your life, I can only imagine."

I stopped eating to question her for the last statement, "What do you mean, Sister Anna?"

She placed her glass down and spoke as if poison was in her mouth, "I'm just saying that you have to deal with demons and all. You stay busy and you

240

have no time for anyone. I am surprised that you are still married, and things are okay, which anything can use improvement."

"My marriage is fine, and my husband understands. We get along great. What would give you the impression that things are just ok?"

"Minister Grace, you stay in your shell, and you never let your hair down. You husband barely sees you and when he does, it's over a bible. I know you have to stay on top of your game and believe God more than the average person. I'm sure Christ did not give us this life for us not to even enjoy ourselves in it. You don't have much fun, a family life, or an earthly life for that matter. Don't be so uptight and frigid. That's all I'm saying. "

I didn't like the way she said that. Some reason, her tone was agitated. I discontinued my food. To test her tone I then spoke, "You are correct. I don't see MY HUSBAND much, but he understands the life WE LIVE. Please don't worry about US. As for those children or any children, it's not even an ISSUE. On the other hand, if I had never STUDIED and DEDICATED my life to helping others, then Christ could not have used ME to deliver YOU and others like YOU on the numerous occasions that I already have. I guess the life I live is helping SOMEONE, SOMEWHERE that appreciates it. By the way, it is FUN and GAMES, when you live in a world that is CORRUPTED with malicious CHAMELEONS that are truly SNAKES that spit POISON VENOM at will."

I must have struck a nerve. She spoke nicely as if to hold back her true meaning. "You're right, but I'm just saying you need to live more life on earth and not concentrate on heaven so much. You do have a husband that has needs."

"Hello ladies."

We both turned our heads toward the doorway and it was my husband's voice that stopped her from exposing her true feelings. He looked at me and walked to me. Before he could get closer, Sister Anna got up and he bumped into her.

"Excuse me."

"No excuse me. I was just getting up to fetch your supper, Bishop."

William walked past her. He kissed me on the cheek, and I spoke, "I can get it, Sister Anna. You have done enough by sharing this gracious meal with us."

"No problem, Minister Grace. You have been tired since you just got up."

"She is right. Let her get the food. I want you to rest."

I gave a nice smile, and Sister Anna went in the kitchen and fixed the plate. She sat him at the opposite end of the table in his usual seat. William prayed over his food and ate it.

"As we were saying, I have always been thankful for your help in deliverance."

I gave her the face because William did not know that Jesus had used me to deliver her from her mess. I never told my husband because she didn't want me to. She stated as her face was towards my husband, "It's okay, Bishop knows. We have no secrets. Isn't that right?"

The word secrets brought back to my mind that there were secrets in our house, and I must tell my husband, but at that moment. It was the way she said, secrets' that gave me an eerie feeling. I then spoke out loud, "What else have you been discussing since I have been in my room, fasting, and praying for the people?"

Before William could say anything, Sister Anna spoke with cheerfulness, "Bishop has been a darling to the children. They just love the piggyback rides he gives them. The way he has been playing and tending to their needs, they can't help but love him. In fact, we all love him. Oh, you too, Minister Grace, not trying to leave you out. Being frank, he has been a gracious host to me and his conversations are dear to me. Above all, I'm almost skeptic about the impending new move."

"What new move?" I asked as if the Lord hadn't already told me because nothing sneaks up on a child of God.

Sister Anna faced William rapidity to say in a slow motion, "Bishop, you haven't told her yet?"

245

I gave my husband that look, and he spoke, "I haven't had the chance and was going to tell her tonight, but since the cats' out the bag, I know it is not a problem."

I gave my husband a confused gaze as I spoke with base, "What is not a problem? Everyone is talking, but I am still listening."

Sister Anna then tore her gawking eyes from my husband. William let out that uncomfortable smirk as he spoke, "I had a discussion with Sister Anna about moving close by. After our discussion, she agreed to sell her house on the other side of town. I opened the doors to our home for her and the children to live here until she can get a place to stay for them."

My ears were still ringing. I could not believe my ears. This man of God had been having conversations with Sister Anna while I have been dealing with things. Not just that, but he decided to let her remain longer in our home without consulting me. Forcing a smile was hard at that time. I said, "Oh. Ok."

The evil in her drank some more of her wine. She even offered William a glass of wine and he shook his hand and his head no. More seconds went by and I was still sitting there trying to rationalize everything.

"It's not a problem is it? The children and I can leave and stay somewhere else until then if we are imposing on your hospitality."

Quick as always to the rescue to make things peaceful, William spoke, "No, Sister Anna, it is not a problem. I hadn't had time to tell her."

They both waited for my answer as they observed me. I then said, "I guess it is alright by me, but what did God say about this decision?"

At first, they did not say a word. Sister Anna said, "I didn't ask God when Bishop and I were discussing this matter. I didn't think I had to ask HIM since this is your earthly home and all."

William continued to sit there as he kept his focus on me. I spoke, "God searches the heart and tries it no matter how evil, deceitful, and wicked it can be."

My husband was quiet for a moment. I knew that he thought of what the revelation of the scripture meant. With a big smile, he leaned forward to say, "That is Jeremiah Chapter seventeen Verses nine and ten, I believe."

Disrupting the way we discuss our differences, Sister Anna got up. She staggered back a bit, and then replied in a crackled, but slurred voice, "If you both excuse me, I believe I will retire and go to bed. It is clear that I am not wanted because I do not understand what you two talking about."

"Wait you don't have to go," my husband stated as he stood up.

I know she pretended not to hear William as she trotted in a slow pace to her room. He waited until she closed the door to reply, "Grace, what you do that for?"

"Me, what I do what for? I was only telling you what the Word says. It is not my fault if she is lacking in the Word and doesn't act like she even wants to know the Word."

"You were quoting scriptures and making her feel uncomfortable."

"Me making her feel uncomfortable. I haven't done anything out of the ordinary. I have not acted in any way that was not right. Here you are telling me that I made her uncomfortable. What about the way she talks to me in my own home, does that not count? Besides, WE always consult God when WE make decisions, this is no different."

I could tell that he was getting a little upset as he spoke tough to me, "You don't have blood family so you can say that. Those children are all I have."

"Blood family? If you think I am going to kiss her butt, you are sadly mistaken. I will not lower who I am just because of family. Blood or not! If you have to be at her every beck and call then fine you do it, but don't come telling me about family. When she has an user spirit operating in her."

"I didn't mean it like that."

"Yes, you did. You meant it the way I took it, but it's ok," I said politely.

"It's just that I have been spending a lot of time with them and I don't want to depart from them."

250

"The children or her?"

"She is there too, but it's been about the children, even the conversations have been about them. Sometimes we would reminisce about my son and her daughter. There has been an occasion that she cries for the loss of her family but that is it."

"Can't you see that the enemy is prying on your weakness, and he doesn't care whom he uses to get the job done."

"What job done?"

"If you both have a connection, then you will start acting on it."

"There is nothing to act on. We only have the children in common."

"That is what I am saying. You two could be together because of the similarities of your lives. Your wife Marsha and her husband both are deceased. Your children died together and left behind two children. Don't you see where I am going with this?"

"I see where you are going, but it is going nowhere with me. Another reason is their house is not safe. I thought why not use this opportunity to bring them closer to me. You should understand there is no one, but us here. Why not have it alive with family?"

I stood up with all kinds of anger rush through me. That was a feeling that I had not ever expressed. Doing my best to remain calm, I answered, "You used personal motives to keep them here, but what about Sister Anna? She deserves a life outside of the children and not just that, she is thinking she has my life."

"Are you serious?"

"You think playing in the enemy's playground is a game? This is real. You have no idea how much that woman wants to be me just to have you and the kids to herself don't you see it?"

"She is beside the point and not an issue to me in my life. As for the children, I understand that, but those children are all she and I have left. I don't plan to depart from them if I don't have to."

"The Word states clearly in the first chapter of JOB that he lost all he had, children, money, but he regained. Don't make the children that important that you idolize them by mistake."

With words barely above a whisper, William stared at me with murky eyes to say, "The money can be replaced, but in this time frame, JOB also had sex to regain the family he had. The only thing I get from you is the Word and a hard time."

I stared at him in disbelief. For the first time, I was started to think that the spouse God gave me was worldlier than anything. He acted selfish and careless of the way we always done things. Tears formed again, but that time it was reality that I did not make my husband happy. I didn't think I was enough, but I believed that God is an on time God and he would supply all of our needs. I made my legs move and William got in my way to say, "Grace, don't be angry. I love you and I didn't mean it. I was just angry and never should have opened my mouth."

I walked off and went upstairs. I talked to myself out loud, "Fine he wants sex, he will get sex."

William came behind me later because he knew I was hurt and upset at our argument. He knew that I only had his best interest at heart and he mine. That night, I decided to be waiting on him and to give him what he really talked about. When he opened the door, I was naked as the day I was born. He stumbled backwards, for shock. He could not take his eyes off my body as he said, "What are you doing?"

"Isn't this what you want? Don't you want a wife that will give you massive sex? Here is my body, take it, and ravish it at your will."

He closed the door behind him and stared at me as if he were stunned to see my character.

"You are not stable or ready for this. Your actions are unlike you and I know it. Sex is the last thing we need to try and do. We have to restore things back to its original state before we can do what you are suggesting."

"How so when you don't know anything?"

"I only know what you told me and that is nothing. You accuse me of strangling you, raping you, and then you are fighting at me in your sleep. What am I to think is happening to you? You preach a good game, but behind those doors you are a wreck waiting to happen. You have to confront whatever it is, and then go from there."

Avoiding what he said I walked seductively closer to him, and said, "Here I am. Isn't this what I have been denying you?"

He swallowed and touched my breast. I was unfeeling for I didn't even feel his touch. He took the opportunity to look into my eyes to murmur, "If you were the same you a few weeks ago, I may jump for joy, but no this is not the way I want it. I want you when you are really ready to give yourself to me and tonight, you are not ready. You are becoming someone I do not recognize anymore. This new you need to go back so the real you can emerge."

"I may not be ready again, if you don't take me tonight. Don't you want to make a rash decision and do what the flesh tells you to do? Don't you want every inch of me?" I pointed back to him.

"You were right earlier. I should have sought God's counsel about asking her to stay, but I listened to the heart. I only saw the children being closer and more convenient. I did not think things through and I was wrong. Lately, things have been out of order and I think I can't help it. As for you not being ready again, then I will just have to wait more years. I love you for you Grace and you're worth the wait."

He pecked my cheek lightly, grabbed his pillow, and blanket. As if he had second thoughts, dropped his head, and closed the door. I continued to stand there. Half-heartedly I was thankful that he did not act on the horny woman I was betraying. Placing my night gown on, I prayed until the Spirit spoke. When I finish the Lord had me to turn to scripture and I saw Matthew

257

Chapter ten Verse sixteen stated, how we will be like innocent sheep among guilty people. We are to watch the enemy and discern as we watch, but not ignorant. I could barely believe it. I sat there flabbergasted because the Lord has confirmed that I must be on guard.

Sister Anna was a predator that lied in wait. I felt it and I didn't want to believe it. As always the Holy Spirit did not lead you wrong, I did not want to think she was up to something because I had been engrossed in my own secrets; therefore, I went to sleep.

Phase 3

In a dream, I went in this hotel to take a shower. A white man had the door blocked as he said, "You don't want to use this bathroom someone tried to break in it and left it all hooked up." Making my eyes look down, I saw that someone had broken into the bathroom, and the locks were still in tack. "There's a bathroom upstairs. You can use that one."

I said thank you and went upstairs. When I got to the bathroom someone was in the first stall, so I went in the second one. Speedily I began to bathe. Soon as I finished, I walked by the first stall and the person said help me. I frowned and began walking, and then urine was all on the floor. I was appalled for it was watery green. Seconds later, blood began to spew over the top stall. In a hurry I made my way almost to the door and another man came in.

He ran over to the stall and started yelling and crying. "Call 9.1.1. quick." I took off and pulled the fire alarm in the building. Moments later the ambulance came and brought out the body, which was cut in half. The police questioned everyone as we lined up in the hall. Before he got to me, I dropped a napkin and this Hispanic man reached to pick it up as I reached down. He said, "What is that on your arm?"

I looked at my right arm and the words, do you trust me? I grabbed my arm and I screamed as I hit his arm. When my eyes opened, I searched my arm for those words; however, they could not be found. Taking a deep breath, I saw I must have fallen asleep at my desk for there were where I awaken. I lightly massaged my neck, it was sore and I assumed I slept crooked. My grandmother taught me that, after a dream if you stayed awake a few minutes you would remember the dream. There I was awake and not knowing what that meant.

Using my hands I wiped my eyes. Getting up I yarned and stretched. I prayed and washed up. That day I would interact with the children, just to keep face. When I made it half way down the stairs, I heard my husband talking to Sister Anna. I sat mid-way to eavesdrop. She said, "I am sorry about getting drunk last night, but I had to. So much has been coming at me and I just needed a little space to breathe."

"We could have watched the children while you relaxed a bit by going somewhere if that would have helped you."

"I know, but I didn't want to go out alone and Minister Grace doesn't do anything, but live and breathe church. Where can we go for fun together?"

"There are a lot of places, like the movies, dinner, or to a spa. Church is her way of life, that is the way she is, and that is the way she stays in tuned with God."

"That is good and all, but I am a lonely woman with two small children to care for all by myself, with no man in sight."

"You won't have to do it alone. We will be there for you."

"How do I know that? You both may be tricking me to move closer just to take them from me by saying I am unfit. I don't have a man, and I haven't had a good sexing in a long time."

"I am sure God will send you the man for you. But, those children mean the world to me and as of now, we wouldn't ever think about taking them from you. You are a great grandmother to them, you do a wonderful job in keeping the house clean, and the meals are spectacular."

She cut him off to spas out, "What about her? Do they mean the world to her? Does she care what I do here?"

He must have walked closer because she seemed to be crying softly. From what I could hear, she sounded to be in his arms. He must have pulled away because I heard her voice say in the same tempo, "I am sorry. I just needed someone to hold me as I cried."

"You feeling better?"

"A little."

"I don't want you to cry. We are here to help you?"

"Do you want me here? I mean do you want me in your life?"

"Sister Anna, we will always have that connection because our children were married and we have grandchildren because of them. Yes, I am glad you are here. You don't need to be alone too often. I'm here for support you and so is my wife."

"I am glad you have opened your arms and heart to me to be near. I am grateful for this moment."

"Sister Anna you are dear to me."

"You smell nice, William."

"Thank you. Now wipe your face and don't worry about custody. You being the primary caretaker is fine. We both agreed on that and that is that."

"What if she doesn't want the children in the house? She seldom comes out, anyway."

"My wife has things she has to do and this is not about Grace. You keep throwing up her to me and like I said this isn't about her. This is about the welfare of the children."

"Yes it is. She will be around them just like we will be. If she doesn't want them around, she can be mean to them and you know children can pick up on things."

"Grace loves them and there is no what if's. No matter what decision is ever to be sought, she and I will seek God about it. Last night, I was in error, and she identified that I was thinking with my mind and not the mind of Christ."

"What about you, William?"

I knew it. I wanted to scream, but a piece of me wanted to see how he would handle himself in a situation like this. Christ had led me to this scripture about being humble but wise. I felt jealous and angry. My hands were trembling as she talked about my husband. My heart raced as I didn't think I could sit still, but I had to. He won't put her in his place because he still got that to work out of him. With a surprise tone, he asked, "What about me?"

"You don't think I know you get lonely. You don't think I know you need earthly companionship. Someone who is on your level and not in the clouds?"

Put that manipulation, seductive, adulterous spirit of Jezebel out. I thought, but he won't because I knew him. He would rather keep peace with her for the children's sake then to tell her to leave. She would hold it over his head and torture him with guilt, until condemnation becomes rooted.

"How I am outside the children is not of your concern. That dissipated a long time ago. Why are you still holding onto the past? I am happily married to a wonderful woman."

"William, William, William, silly William. You always put others needs ahead of your own. That is one of the qualities that I admire in you, but when are you going to satisfy your need that I know you have?"

"My wife does that just fine. How we get off you getting drunk and the kids to my wife and my needs?"

"I'm just asking questions."

"You are asking questions about the wrong thing, Sister Anna."

"You use to call me Anna. Do you remember the times or have you forgotten?"

"That was a time in my life before I met my wife."

Deciding I had, had enough. I yelled out, "William, you downstairs?"

"Right here."

I slightly got up and walked down the stairs slowly. When I reached the bottom, Sister Anna was on the couch, pretending to be asleep. Putting a fake smile on my face was hard to do, but I managed it. William asked so tenderly, "What you need?"

I knew she was listening. It was wrong to play, but I could not resist the urge to give her something to listen too. I said, "Babe we must be wise as serpents and humble as doves. The Lord gave me that last night. But, I like the terms, a wolf in sheep's clothing."

"A wolf in sheep's clothing, humble as doves, wise as serpents, what you think it all means?" He asked with sincerity.

"Maybe we need to kick the bond woman out Abram."

"Abram?"

I knew I had his attention because of the way his eyebrow curl upward when we speak of the Word. He knew that when I spoke of the Word, I was not of myself. As quickly as I spoke the name Abram, the Lord dealt with me. Instantly, it was for him. Forgetting about Sister Anna, I permitted the Holy Spirit to use me, "In the Old Testament, Abram name was changed to Abraham once he became a new creature. Other than that, Abraham was in need of the promise son. Instead he went to the bondwoman and produced Ishmael. To be tested of his faith, he was told to sacrifice the promise seed, which was Isaac. You lost your son, Daniel, and you can't make Daniel Jr. your promise seed. He will never be an heir the way you want him to. Also I believe in Galatians four and thirty the scripture says: the woman of bondage and her family must not be with the woman that is free and her family. The family that is not right will not have the things of God."

"Where you going with this?"

"The promise seed must come forth, in due season, and he can't come forth if there is a son here."

Sister Anna began to mumble as to break up the conversation. I spoke to read his countenance, "Do you get it?"

He looked at her and spoke in a discreet tone, "We can talk about this later."

It somewhat bothered me because he knew she was not asleep. He knew that I had a feeling that she was not asleep. Detesting the fact that he played like putty in her hand made me ill. Never had such emotions rose in me like now. Wrapping my arms around William I spoke teasingly. "Ok, later. Where you off to now?"

"I have the day off and I'm going to spend it with the children."

"I would tag along, but use this time to bond more with them without Sister Anna and me around."

"What you going to do today?"

"I need to be praying for the people that latch onto things that are not of God."

"Do what you have to."

"Ok. Peace and quiet sounds wonderful. Guess I will go in the downstairs study."

"I love you, Grace Dalton."

"I love you too, William Dalton."

He gave me a kiss and left out. I continue to stand in hope she would move, but she did not. She continued to lie there. I felt within my spirit that the time was not right for the two of us to have a conversation. Soon as he left, I went in the study

271

downstairs. I placed outside my do not disturb sign and began my reading. It didn't feel like hours had past, but soon as I began to pray, I could hear Sister Anna, singing at the top of her lungs. It was a beautiful song no doubt, but not at that moment. I knew she was purposely doing that so I couldn't reach God like I wanted to. The devil knew when to attack and who to use to help in his attack.

For a while I sat there. For the first time in a long time I cried. Things she said were right. I don't know anything about being a mother. I have never had the desire to be one. Partially because of what I saw as a child or how I was treated. My grandparents showed me love, but their main objective was to prepare me for the enemy. Going out, drinking, and all those other things have never been me. I don't desire for those things now. I just want to be a great wife to William and if it is meant, the rest will come later. For the life of me, it is unparalleled to have a husband that I don't know how to please, physically.

The more I thought about it the harder I cried out. The more I cried out, the more I drowned out her singing. When I finished crying and praying, I closed the bible. The Word in my spirit was Love, love, love. It had never occurred to me of what I had to do. I have to allow myself to be loved, physically, and emotionally by anyone. My entire life had been devoted to God, which wasn't bad, but what about the life HE had given me to live? Oddly enough, HE would not have deemed it fit for me to be in a marriage if I could not love or consummate.

Anything outside the Word, I would be lost. This is a new experience for me; although, I was married for three years. I still had not outwardly showed my husband love. On the other hand, I knew William loved me, but to feel it, was different. I realized that I didn't know how to give love and I didn't know how to receive love. The fact made me cry. I sat there and cried like a baby in need of its mother for comfort. The more I cried the more I thought about the child I bore. How innocent the child appeared on that stage. I cried more for I saw the way he was sacrificed to Molech.

I could not change the past or what happened in it. Before I could be honest with my future with William there were many things in my past that I must tell him. It was so long ago, I thought as I cried my heart out to God. Why didn't I reject my fate? I asked within myself. No answer I heard pleased me and the Holy Spirit took over. I began to repent of my sins in the spirit as the word marriages kept coming up.

When I awoke to a quiet house I smiled. I got up and my cell phone rang. I did not recognize the number, but I felt the need to answer it.

"Hello."

"Is this Minister Grace Dalton?"

"Yes this is she. May I ask who is calling?"

"This is the secretary at the Blood of Jesus United Methodist Church. You are scheduled to speak next week, but due to a misprint of time, you are scheduled to come in this evening. Can you make it on such a short notice?"

"About what time?"

"Around seven."

I saw the time was five fifteen. I calculated that it would take thirty minutes to get there and glad it wasn't farther than that. I spoke, "Yes, I can make it today."

"Great. We look forward to hearing what God has to say. Goodbye."

"Goodbye."

The air in the house was cooler. I thought it is too cool for the children, but to each its own. Sister Anna was in the living room and she turned over to see me.

"You still asleep?"

"Yeah I was. I thought you were Bishop bringing the children back."

"No they are still out. Is it cool enough in here for you? It feels too cool for me."

"No it feels great in here and the children love the cool."

William opened the door with the children in tow. He spoke, "Hey, I'm home."

We both said, "Yes."

Sister Anna smiled, and said, "I thought he said Anna, I'm home."

"No ma'am he said, "Hey, I'm home."

Not going to be provoked to anger as I turned to face the children. Surprisingly enough they came to me screaming, "Grandma, grandma we had fun today."

I could feel the anger that Sister Anna had as her eyes beat me in the back of the head. I spoke, "That is wonderful children. Now go tell Grandma Anna about your day as well."

They went over to her as William came over to me. I said, "You know the church I supposed to preach at next week."

"Yeah what about it?"

"They called and need me to come in today. I told them yes."

"Ok. Give me a few and I will get ready so we can go."

"You don't have to go. I know you are tired and need some rest."

He gave me the look of, I don't think I should stay. I spoke, "If you want to go come on. Don't complain to me if you are tired in the morning."

Before we could make our way upstairs, Daniel Jr. came over and said, "Grandpa Will, can you read me a story?"

He looked at me and I spoke, "Sure he can, as soon as he comes back downstairs."

We went upstairs and I said, "You know she had him to do that, don't you?"

"Maybe, but we didn't see her do it, so we can't say it was her doing. The child might want a story read to him and it's innocent."

"Before she came here, I might have thought so, but since her stay here, all she does is have motives. How can you not see it?"

"I am not looking for anything else. The children are all I see."

Right then I decided to let him know that I knew she was up to no good. I stated back to him her words for word, "William, William, William, silly William. You always put others needs ahead of your own. That is one of the qualities that I admire in you, but when are you going to satisfy your need that I know you have."

His eyes observed me as I stated that phrase. He said, "You were listening to us talk?"

"Yes and I also noticed, how she plays on your weakness."

"You were listening to us talk?"

"Yes! I was listening to you both talk. You think I was wrong?"

"Yes, you were wrong."

"Ok, I might be, but when are you wrong when it comes to her and the children? Foolish church man who has you twisted?"

"I am not bewitched, bound, or twisted in no shape, Grace. I can't believe you were listening to us talk."

"You weren't going to tell me, and then you played along with it by letting her pretend to be asleep."

"I know you didn't believe she was asleep for the Holy Ghost will not let a spirit led child walk into traps, unaware."

"So, you know that the spirit in me tells me that she is after you and wants me gone."

"Grace at one point in time I might have believed it, but now I don't. She is not after me. You are just jealous and can't understand the human emotions you are now expressing."

"Human emotions, that I am now expressing and jealousy? Are you even listening to yourself talk? The enemy is in the form of Anna and the children. He is using them to get to you and to break us up."

"Anna I can understand, but how has she used the children to come between us?"

"Like tonight, I know she wants you so bad she can literally taste you. It doesn't look right with you and her here alone so she has the boy whom favors your son so much to ask you to read a story. This means you can't come with me. After the story is read, the two of you will be alone and you never trust a desperate woman."

"Grace listen to what you are saying. Do you even know how ridiculous it sounds coming from your lips?"

"I haven't slept with you willingly, but here in my own house is a woman that is desperate to give you what you want. You and I have no earthly ties. The two of you have a family history. Tell me where does this leave me? Make me believe that you don't believe me?" He did not answer as I went on to say, "It leaves me out in the cold."

"How so? You won't even tell me about your past. All I know is the great and powerful, powerhouse speaker, preacher, teacher, Apostle, Prophet Grace Dalton. I don't know anything else but that. So, when you going to tell me what I need to know about your life before Christ?"

He was right, but I could not get into it. I have to speak to God's people in an hour or so. I didn't need to get into a disagreement. Politely I said, "When God is ready for you to know, you will know when I know, but to be honest I don't even know."

"That's a cop out, Grace, and you know it."

"Right now, I have to speak and I can't get into anything more than that with you."

He understood as he went downstairs. I began to pray again and that time, I got ready and went downstairs. William was not there. Sister Anna was at the table with the children as usual, feeding them and drinking her wine. I bid my goodbyes and left for the speaking engagement. The Blood of Jesus United Methodist Church, Incorporate was a different type of church. They have half naked praise dancers and all kinds of festivities going on, all year round. In this

283

church, the women outnumbered the men and three fourth the churches were single. They believed in the new age dating, premarital sex, and everyone in the church had been divorce or in a process of getting one. To top it off, it is a family church.

I didn't care to speak in family churches, but the Lord placed the church in my path months before. They didn't believe in women speaking and I didn't care to give what was Holy to the dogs. Just so happen, the woman they had speaking got sick and could not be in their program. Because she recommended me, the door of opportunity opened and I gladly accepted. The main thing was every speaker had about ten minutes to speak about whatever they choose. It was out of the ordinary to me, but this is how they do things. However, I was to speak as the Spirit gave utterance. They didn't know what the Lord would have me to say, but whatever it was, I was sure it w would be much needed to those that were hungry.

When I arrived, they ushered me to sit upfront along with the other speakers outside the pulpit to watch the half-naked women danced, flaunting their bodies in front of the men and impressionable young boys. I thought the women and young girls could have put on more clothes, but that was not my church house. The choir brought forth songs to make the flesh move because I did not feel the spirit anywhere. It was like a show being put on for the weak because the next week the same show went to another church across state line.

I would speak on something easy so I can go home. After dead speakers spoke on various topics, I began to speak within, Lord I need to give these people a Word from on High. I could speak about giving money, being faithful to the church, and so on like the rest of the speakers but they don't need to hear about stuff these others are already saying. When the Mistress of Ceremony called my name and they all stared at me and at that moment, I knew my topic. Out loud with such a tone I called out, "Praise God, everyone."

They responded, "Praise God."

"Yes, the Lord is worthy to be praised every day. I won't be before you long, but it's however, the Lord uses me to be honest with you. After listening to all the speakers that have gone before me, I asked the Lord to give me a Word for your soul and HE did. I am thankful to be able to be in the presence of the Lord as I speak what I believe is the Word HE has for you. Tonight, I am going to give you food for thought. Any woman can be a girlfriend, but not any woman can be a wife. It takes more than attracting the man, you have to keep him, and you can't keep him without God working

286

in it. There are too many girlfriends looking for a boyfriend and not enough boyfriends looking for a wife. There are too many people breaking commitments and not enough people making commitments. Everyone wants the date now, marry later theory of love. My grandmother Tillie use to tell me why would a man buy the cow when he can get the milk for free? Basically, she was saying, why a man would marry a woman if he is getting everything he wants without a ring. He is getting honesty, faithfulness, trust, sex, money, children, and commitment. He is getting what a married man gets without going before God and that is not right. What are his actions really saying to you? Is he saying, I love you, but not enough to give you my last name? By you agreeing, what are telling him? I can tell you, that you are telling him that you love him enough to stay in sin? Maybe you like the idea of just having a boyfriend and not a husband? By not getting married and just shacking, you get caught up, and before you know it, you agree with the sins. You agree it's ok to not get married and you agree to be done in part. If you are truly seeking Christ for a mate, he will send him to you. In Proverbs eighteen and twenty-two it did not say women go looking for him. He will find you. But, God can't give HIS good men to you, if you are a wreck. You have to clean yourself up and go back to your first love, which, is God. I once heard that Christian marriages have the highest divorce rate. It is simply because in "supposed to be" Christian marriages, there is too much flesh and not enough Spirit. The truth is, too many Christian marriages are chasing after the things in this world and not the things of God. They have accepted the way the world do things in marriages and that is why they fail. They don't want to be singled out, so they try to fit in and that is their biggest mistake. Most of the time, women will get with the first man that says he is of God. They run with it because they are lonely or just want to be with someone. They assumed that if I am a Christian, God will work through my marriage and save him because the believing wife is able to sanctify the unbelieving husband or vice versa. The difference is, God can, but is it God's Will? If true Christians listen to God and not their own minds, divorce would not be an option. The bottom line is we have too many girlfriends and not enough wives. You all pray my strength in the Lord."

I walked to my seat. The church was quiet and the other speakers appeared stunned for the way the Lord used me to speak to HIS people. No one said a word not even the children. For over three minutes, no one spoke, clapped or made a sound. The mistress of

289

ceremony finally got up to speak and she was without words at first. She cleared her throat and whispered slowly, "Let's give Minister Grace Dalton, an applause, for the Word of God."

The people clapped, but not a hearty clap. I didn't expect it because the Word cuts. The other speakers were entertaining the flesh with their words of prosperity, but not I. The rest of the show was cut short because those after me claimed they were led to just pray for the people. When the show was over, a man came to me, and spoke, "You Grace McBride from the compound, in Utah?"

I haven't heard that in a long time and I didn't think people knew. For years, Christian people called me Minister Grace and when I got married I was still Minister Grace. Some added Dalton and some didn't. However, I was taken aback to hear that name.

"Yes, who are you?"

"I am Warden Jeremiah Prickly. I run the prison over in Utah."

"I don't believe I know you."

"No ma'am you don't, but a few months ago an inmate was sliced in half."

My first thoughts went back to my dream and how I saw the man cut in half. I then responded, "What does that have to do with me?"

"In his possession was a letter addressed to you. I brought it with me, but it is at my hotel room. If you come by the Hilton, I will leave it out front. I'll have to get you to sign for it."

"That won't be a problem."

"I'm glad because no one has heard of you, and we have searched data bases, and you are a mystery. I was beginning to think that you did not exist. No schools had ever heard of you, and I remembered the man said you might be a preaching. What do you know you are?"

"I was home schooled by my mother's parents, the McBride's. We moved from Utah to Louisiana."

"Well, that explains it. I will have the letter taken downstairs as soon as I get back. You will have to show your ID before you get it, ok?"

"That is not a problem."

"Good, I am glad to finally get this letter to its rightful owner."

"How did you know I am the one?"

"The description fits you and I honestly didn't know. I actually took a chance and glad I am a gambling man. Oh, by the way, awesome words, coming from a gal like you."

"Thank you."

He tilted his hat in a southern style and left. I just stood there puzzled and not knowing what to think. I got in my car and drove home. I was anxious and being anxious was something we were not to be. During the drive home, I could think of nothing, but the letter. I don't know why I did not ask who it was from and how long had he had it. I was thrown back when he said from the compound. My own husband does not know about my life. It wasn't because I kept if from him. I kept it from me, but the way things escaladed I better make up my mind to tell him. For now I need to know for myself.

When I made it home, a strange awareness crossed me. With my heart in my chest, jumping all over the place, I took into account that the lights were dim. For a brief moment, I thought William had a late night dinner cooked like he used to, but quickly

293

dismissed that. Turning the knob, I was surprised to find it unlocked. I opened the front door and it did not make a sound. I was going to ease upstairs and not wake anyone, but the Spirit of God told me to turn on the lights. When I did, it proved to be a fleshly bad idea. Lying there asleep on the huge couch was my husband and in William's arms was no other than Sister Anna.

I wanted to melt away because I was gripped by a feeling that I had never experienced before. Nothing in the Word of God could have prepared me for the sight that encompassed my vision. An evil emotion stood up in me and I could feel it, just like I could feel the Holy Spirit. Something unreal had a hold of me. It disagreed with me, but I did not listen to the Holy Spirit. I snatched her up off my husband before I could blink my eyes. William woke up and stated with such a surprise, "Grace, I fell asleep rocking the children to sleep." I ignored him and Sister Anna did not say a word. I walked up the stairs with tears. I didn't even know I had. He came behind me to say, "It's not what you think?"

Undressing, I still did not say a word. I didn't think I needed to. He continued to say, "Babe talk to me. It's not what you think."

I stopped undressing to say, "If it's not what I think, tell me what it is you think I think?"

"You think I was holding her as I slept."

"That's not what I think. That is what I saw."

"You think I been with her."

"That's not what I think that is what I am beginning to think."

"I fell asleep holding the children. I didn't know it was her until you came home. That is the honest truth."

"Then you need to explain to her that you don't want her and that you are married to me."

"I don't have to explain that. She knew I didn't want her and I'm married to you. That's nonsense. Where are all these feelings coming from?"

"Oh, ok continue to be unlearned if you must, but she has to go."

"She and the children are not going anywhere. They don't have a place close by yet and I will not throw my family out on the street."

"Not throw your family out on the street. Throw her out on the street."

"How can you be of God and speak things as you are?"

"How can you be of God and not see what the enemy is trying to do?"

"Well I am not throwing them out."

"Fine, don't."

I didn't say another word. I could not say a word. William was being blinded and didn't realize it. He stormed out the room and went back downstairs. One can only assume, he was with her and I was up her alone and wondering. I refused to cry. I refused to be sad because that was all I have been doing since the day Sister Anna and the children came to my house. The next day, I woke up somewhat rested. Then, my mind went back to the letter the man. I was nervous and I didn't know why. I didn't know what to think, but I knew that if I didn't go, I would wonder for the rest of my life. Getting up, William kneeled in front of the recliner praying.

He did not hear me get up because I was quiet as possible. I stood there and listen. He spoke in tongue. For the first time in a while, my husband had his face to the floor and seeks God for counsel. I pray it was about Sister Anna and the children. I hoped he listened to the spirit and not his flesh. I wrote him a small note stating that I have to run uptown and would be back in a few. When I got downstairs, Sister Anna was sitting at the table. She said, "I'm sorry about falling asleep in William's arms. It was not what it appeared to be."

"That is what it appeared to be."

"I respect you. I got a little tipsy while watching William play with the children and that was it."

"Look, I have to go uptown and I don't have time to chit chat. Please excuse me."

"Could I tag along? I need to get out for a spell."

I figured why not? That way she wouldn't be near my husband, and I could hear what was really in her heart. "Sure, where are the children?"

"They are asleep and about time he comes downstairs they will already be up. Besides, I had already told Bishop that I would like to go uptown. You know, have girl time, just you and I. He thought that was a great idea since the children will know us both as grandmother. Well they will address me as Grandma Anna and you, how about Me Maw Grace?"

"Call me Me Maw Grace?" I questioned her back.

"Perfect. I knew you would like that besides it fits you better than me. Let me grab my purse and I am set."

We got in the car and began our journey uptown. I usually didn't listen to music, but decided to listen to the Family Worship Center Choir CD. Sister Anna did not say a word. She was different that day. She sang along with the songs, and she was being pleasant. I arrived to the hotel, and she spoke, "Why we at a hotel. What gives?"

"I have to pick up a letter at the front desk."

"Oh."

She said oh with naughty intentions because of the smirk on her face. I on the other hand paid it no mind. I am just nervous about reading what someone wrote to me. Parking the car, Sister Anna waits for me as I enter the lobby. I showed my ID and sign for the letter. I was nervous all over again plus that man was the first to ever mention the compound. I had never thought of whatever happened to it or the people left in it. All I knew was, I made it out and my mom died that night.

300

On my way back to the car, I saw Sister Anna hanging up her cell. I got in the car and asked bluntly, "So, what did William want or what did you tell him when you called him?"

"What makes you think it was Bishop?"

"There has not been a conversation about another man since the day you set foot in my home. Why would it not be him?"

"You are too funny, and it was Bishop. I told him you were in the hotel getting a letter and he asked what hotel and I told him."

"Oh, ok. Thank you."

"I wasn't in error was I?"

"You know when you are in error. That much I am sure."

She gave me a smile that was sure underhanded. I did not give her the pleasure of knowing that I was

301

upset about her telling my husband my business before I had a chance to. However, I pretended that all was well and she bought it. The rest of the day went by without any misunderstandings. I didn't get a chance to read the letter; although, I was more than ready, but not with her around.

We arrived back to my house and William, and the children had cooked lunch. I felt like crying because everything that was said either pointed to William or Sister Anna. They on the other hand mainly talked to the children. I was invisible. No matter how I tried to include myself in the conversations, she always found a way to exclude me. She was in my house, acting like the belle of the ball. On other words, she laughed and carried on, doing her best to make me feel like an outsider. Little did she know, I wanted to be alone to read the contents of the letter.

Seizing the opportunity to leave, I excused myself and went upstairs. William offered to help her clean up. After that evenings' show at the Dalton Family Extended, I finally decided to give up trying to make him see her for the devil I knew she was. It was in God's hands to open the eyes of my blinded husband. Before I could close the door, I heard Sister Anna laughing as if William said the funniest thing. I thought, he had never made me laugh like that before. Sensing a tear, I wiped it away as quickly as it started. It is too early to go to bed, but I decided to change into my night clothes, anyway. I sat beside the bed and read with nerves.

Dear Gracie,

I know you are wondering who I am and why am I writing you. I know you are wondering who has contacted you after all these years. I didn't think you could be found and honestly, if you have this letter than I have been cut in half for my sins.

Immediately I thought about the dream I had the other night. I began to tremble as I searched for my breath. Taking a moment from the letter I started walking around the room to regain normal breathing. Settling back down, I picked up where I left off.

The last time I saw you alive, you and your mother were escaping out the side passage. I deeply regretted not going with you both, but my duty then was to fight for heaven. However, I knew that if you escaped that you would be preaching and being an idealist just like her. How I miss you both over the years.

When the invaders, you know the English people came in all the women and children were to drink of the poisonous drink and die as we die. All the women did their duty and we still lost. Many of us were

killed, but a few of us lived. All your brothers died in
this so called Holy war even Majesty Leader.

I could no longer hold back the tears. I cried silently as I sank on my bed. Literally all the strength was gone out of me and I did not know if I could stop spiraling downward. There I was reading a letter from my father. Whom I thought was deceased and he told me that he had been alive all of that time. I sensed the presence of being robbed. Deciding to read more I sat up, dried my eyes, and read: *First thing first, I went to prison and served a very long time for all the crimes they say was against us. I also had my own crimes for interfering with justice, resisting arrest, plain assault, and aggravated assault on police. I was so use to living in the comfort of walls that being on the outside was not for me. I got arrested again and finally ended up here in this prison.*

Second, Majesty Leader was your brother and I
dreaded that fact. Back then I believed in what I was
doing and what the Majesty Leader before him taught
him. I knew you became smitten with him, even at that
young of an age, but I could not do anything about it.
Sadly enough, he fell in love with you.

He loved me? He really loved me? I kept saying
over and over because I could not believe it. I cried
more all the more, for a love that is frowned upon
through the New Testament. The one man that touched
my life, my heart was actually my blood brother. Not
only did he touch my life, but he loved me as well. That
accusation alone hurt to the core of my soul. I know it
didn't sound right, but at the age of a young child
nothing mattered.

The more I forgot about my life before the age
of eleven, the more I remember. All of these emotions

have been bottled up and presumed to have been thrown away. For the faintest idea, I never knew he was my oldest brother, family for that matter. I swallowed hard as I began to read more.

I don't know what happened between the two of you, but he wanted to marry you and raise your son together. But, the Elders of the church we would not forbid it, in fear of jeopardizing our eternal passage. I even knew it was wrong to allow such a meeting between siblings to take place, but I was blind and in the Spirit of Error like your mother told me. Its funny how I believed all your mother said that night we discussed about you being the chosen one. I didn't want to, but when I lived as an Englishman, to attract your mother, I learned about Jesus and what HIS Word says.

Once I came back home to the compound, I had to adapt back down to their ways. Truthfully I had no intentions of really falling for her, but I did. I truly

loved her and it grieved her, so when your

grandparents rejected me due to my age. Your mother

was so immovable about letting the devil have you.

Strange as it is, I knew she would take the chance to

leave and she did. What happened to her, your

grandparents never did say, but I am glad you know

who Jesus is and not being shaken like I or your mother

once was.

Third, you are wondering why I did not contact

you. I had contacted your grandparents and told them

to tell you I was sorry. I also said that I did not want to

see you because I was embarrassed and ashamed about

falling for the trick of the enemy. It took all these years

and losing all my children to realize that your mother

was right. All that talk she did about Jesus was right.

When I come to the knowledge of this I decided the only

thing I could do was to live a life of solitude and that is

what I did.

Last of all, the compound is all rubbles now. I

think they finished taking it down and put up shopping

malls. The house you lived in for eleven years stands no

more. In its place, I believe is some type of building.

Like you, I have tried to put the past behind me and go

on. But, unlike you, it has been difficult with so many

unanswered questions. Believe me, daughter when I say

I love you and I have accepted Jesus as my Lord and

Savior. I love you beyond measure. I hate that I never

told you this in person, but back then times were

different. I was different.

Finally, do you tre' me? That was your mother

way of saying do you trust me? Gracie, I trusted her

like I have always trusted you and glad that you are

more like your mother than me. I hope to see you in the

real Heaven with our real Lord and Savior Jesus Christ of Nazareth.

Love,

Your earthly Father James

I folded the letter up and sat there unfeeling and dismayed. Many things had happened in my life and there I was with a decision to make. If I told him of my past, would he leave me, or if I didn't tell him of my past he would leave me? Those questions baffled me and for the life of me I did not want him to leave my life. Because I knew God and I knew that nothing happened without his prior knowledge and that HE expected me to do what was right. I also was aware of lies and what held back secrets could do to a relationship, a marriage, altogether.

Folding the letter, I went downstairs to talk to William. I would not be held hostage in my own mind

310

by what I thought. Wanting answers and not getting them was the worst kind of battle that you could fight. It was always the inward man that seeks what the flesh desired to know. Upon arriving downstairs, William was gone. I assumed that the happy family was gone to get supper. Before I could face the kitchen, I froze. From behind me I heard a sound I haven't heard since the days of my mother. It was the sound of a snake hissing. The Holy Spirit told me to move and when I did, Sister Anna leaped towards me.

In haste, I moved out the way and she fell towards the floor. She got up and squared at me. I did not move. She then spoke like a snake, "Preacher, Preacher, Preacher. What's wrong? You hear something you recognize?"

"I command you, Slufoot, to lose her soul in the name of Jesus by the blood of the Lamb."

311

She moved slowly like a snake toward me as she said, "He is not going anywhere. He has legal rights to be here."

"Sister Anna you are a child of God and cannot be possessed. Satan has no authority to live in your body. Hear me and reject him."

"Preacher, you are wrong. She sold her soul to me, like your mother did."

I heard a sound and saw that it was William and the children pulling up. Quickly I knew the children could not see their grandmother in this possessive state. I knew that emps, Satan's little demons, didn't like to be cornered and I didn't have ample time to help her. Remembering that important information I stated, "I corner you, Satan, in the name of Jesus. You will stay put until the appointed time for her deliverance.

Matthew twenty seven and sixty six states: placing you in a grave with a stone in front that is watched."

The evil spirit in Sister Anna screamed out, "You can't do this."

"I just did in Jesus name."

With that she fell onto the floor and wiggled. Soon as she stopped moving she passed out. I went to her side to put her on the couch so it would look like she was sleeping. When I made it to her side and began dragging her to the couch, the door swung open and they all stopped. I looked up and all eyes were on me. William put Carla Ann down. He looked at me, and then at Sister Anna. Without thinking about the words he was about to speak, he yelled at me, "What have you done to her?"

"What have I done to her?"

All I could do was re-ask the question. The children then sensed something must be wrong so they came towards us, crying hysterically. William was behind them. They all ran past me and went to her. My thoughts were all my thoughts. I couldn't believe that he thought I had done something to her. How could he have imagined that I would hurt a soul? I took my tears along with my droopy head and went to the back yard patio. I sat there for almost three hours before any sign of life knew I was gone. The door opened and I saw that it was William. Across his shoulder was a blanket and in his hands were coffee mugs. I turned my head from him because I did not want him to see me cry.

He placed the mugs on the patio table and placed the blanket across me. Without saying a word, he lit the outside fire pit, and sat beside me. I still did not look at him nor did I speak. He spoke, "I was frantic today when I saw Sister Anna stretched out like that. It wasn't until I looked at her eyes to know that you were in the middle of delivering her."

I was still quiet as he spoke more, "I am sorry, Grace. So sorry. I consciously know that you would not harm her, but it did not look like that." I guess he waited on me to say something, but I would not. He got in front of me and solemnly asked, "Could you ever find it in your heart to forgive me?"

So much rushed through my mind at him. How could he have thought that I would hurt her? Knowing God's Word like I did, I glanced up at him, and silently stated, "Yes, I can forgive you."

William then became more apologetic than ever. I heard him, but I wasn't listening to him. He noticed that I was still silent. He touched my hands and whispered, "Grace, what's wrong?"

Tears flowed down my cheek and sniffles escaped my mouth. I finally remember the past and had to face it. Easing the tears I replied, "I had come downstairs because I believe that it was time for me to tell you what I recalled from my life, but you were gone. I actually thought you all were gone until I heard the hissing coming from behind me. Soon as I turned around she reached out for me to hit me, but I moved out the way. Sister Anna allowed the enemy to speak through her."

I was quiet as I waited for him to speak.

"I saw the way her eyes had rolled back and you delivering her came to mind. I would have come out earlier, but I took care of the children while she was still down and you were out here. Grace, babe I know. I have always known, but the sight looked ungodly."

"I see."

"It's not to say that you were. It was the sight in general."

Breathing in deeply, I continued, "She has sold her soul to the devil and if she does not release the contract she has with him, I nor you can help her. She will begin to have mind problems and before we know it, a danger to herself and the children."

"I know you are right."

"Back to what I have to say. I could not tell you about my past because I did not know about my past. I could not possibly tell you what I did not know and now that I do, I am facing my past in order to protect my future."

The more, I sat there and told him everything, he cried like I did. I had never thought of him as being so understanding. I knew he would understand, but never had I thought he would understand me as he did.

William was compassionate as he relentlessly listened to me tell him the story of me. He never once judged me, nor did he look at me any differently. If anything he has learned a new appreciation of me and that means so much to me. I never knew how broken I was until I let it all come out tonight. I had no idea just how much I had pushed to the back of my mind until it all came rushing out.

We talked about my life and how God worked through our situations to make us better if not stronger. He provoked me to good works just by his conversation with me. William proved to be more than a help meet. He proved to be just the friend I needed when I needed him.

Before I went upstairs to sleep, William was still sitting in the same spot. He said, "I now fully understand you more now than I had ever. I realize what it is I need to do and by helping you I got the help I needed. Go on to bed and when you awake, we will talk."

"I thought I had talked out," I said with a faint smile.

"You have I haven't."

I closed the door and made my way upstairs. I had a new outlook for people that got delivered. It was truly awesome once you cry out to God and let go of things that held you hostage. My past was holding me and I had no clue that I was in a form of jail until that night. Easing upstairs, I took off my clothes and for the first time, I slept naked and not afraid of any ghost that may haunt me. Nothing crossed my mind, but sleep. It was the kind of sleep that made you want to sleep forever without being bothered by anyone.

However, I awoke the next evening feeling better than ever. I had cried out so much that I was literally weak. I listened as I did not hear a sound. That was odd. The quietness alarmed me and I got up. Grabbing my robe, I wrapped up and went downstairs. The house was clean and my house felt like my house, but with more love. It was then that I realized that I did love my husband. All my life, I had been missing real love. I had never had love and what I felt at a child was infatuation and that feeling wasn't even felt anymore. I felt tingly all over and it had me smiling and excited about seeing William come home. I didn't know that love could feel like that.

That was a new area for me to explore and to think, it took me over forty years to find out, God's plan for me. I smiled then remembered that no one was there. I looked in the room and no Sister Anna. Going over to the window, I peeped outside to the swing set that William bought for the children, no children. I was beginning to become weary. My mind continued to ramble as to find the people that are not here. Moments later a cab pulled up outside. I saw that it was Sister Anna. She came to the door and knocked. *Why is she knocking,* I thought as I loudly yelled, "Come in."

She walked through the door and stood there as if I were the enemy. I said, "Good morning."

"What's so good about it?" Was her reply.

"You are still alive that is what's so good about it."

"I see."

"Sister Anna, what happened?"

"I just come to get a few things, William took us away so we can't disturb his lovely frigid wife."

"I didn't know he took you all out the house."

"Excuse me, let me go in the room and get a few things. I will be right out. I have a taxi waiting on me."

She went in the room and came out as quickly as she went in. In her possession was a nightgown and nothing more. Sister Anna glared at me with an evil look. She looked me up and down, and then walked a circle around me like she was checking me out. Making her way back to my face, she declared, "You think you are so much better than me don't you?"

"How is that?"

"You have the husband."

"You can have one when God is ready for you to have one." When she lowered her gaze, I knew that the enemy was speaking through her and they can't stand to have a Godly person look in the eyes. I used the opportunity to say, "Look at me, Sister Anna."

"She is not here," the voice spoke in a taunting tone.

" Look at me. I am led by God to pray for you. I know you don't want to live like this."

"Help me, Minister Grace," was her frail weak fleshly tone.

"Before I can help you, you have to denounce all legal rights and repent."

I prayed and the Spirit of the Lord took over. Like never before, I prayed for her soul and when I came to, Sister Anna got in the taxi and left. She again had left half delivered and was faced with more critical need of being helped. Loudly I proclaimed, "Lord, I have done my duty. I have tried to deliver her and each time Lord, she evades your Will. I decree that her blood is no longer required at my hands and nor are her actions. In Jesus name, Amen."

323

I lay on the couch, again exhausted, and overwhelmed. Sometime later I heard, "Grace, honey wake up. We need to talk."

Groggily in my view, there was William. I smiled like never before. Tenderly he touched my face as I sat up. "What time is it?"

"Babe, its seven p.m."

"Wow. I slept all day then."

"It appears so."

"Sister Anna came by today."

Sitting beside me he spoke, "What did she want?"

"She said she came to get a few things and how they don't live here anymore. The Spirit of the Lord led me to pray for her and during prayer, her deliverance started. She was indeed willing, but her flesh took over and she took flight."

324

" I know you will do all you can and that is all you can do."

"You right, but I hate to see God's people held captive when they don't have to."

"That is a choice they have to make. You can't make it for them. If you could I know you would."

"When did she and the children move out?"

"When you went up to bed. I thought longer on what you had told me."

"And?"

"And, do you remember when I told you that by helping you, it helped me?"

"Yeah you did tell me that but how?"

"I was going after the flesh. I was still distraught in some form about my son. You were right when you told me I was trying to make my grandson, my son. I had never looked at it like that, but that is what it is. It took you to open my eyes to it. I realized that I must let go, spiritually. I knew that it would not be easy, but I did not want to let go."

He cried and I was moved by what all happened to us. I poured out my soul to him the night before and there he was pouring out his soul to me. I could truly see God at work and it was amazing to see things come together and fitting like it needs to.

" I sat Sister Anna down and told her that she has to go and how I was led by the flesh and my feelings to allow my own personal interest of my grandchildren to get in the way of my life with my wife."

I used my gown to wipe away his tears. He looked at me and stated, "I have loved you with all my heart and I was blind to my own sin. I never thought that anything was done wrong, but it was. I was wrong for not believing you and for putting my own needs of my grandchildren ahead of you. Ahead of the woman God gave me. I was stubborn and did not want to listen, even when I knew you were telling me the truth. It just hurt to hear it spoken to me out loud. It pained me to know that you were right and how wrong I was. Thank you Grace for doing that. Thank you Grace for being you."

"Oh, William. It means so much to hear you say that you listened."

"It's not just that Grace, I was to start a relationship with Anna."

My eyes bucked. I was stunned because all I heard was relationship with Anna. I got up and asked, "Please explain."

"When our children died, we thought that it would be the right thing to do. We thought that us living as a couple was right even if it didn't feel right."

"Did you sleep with her?"

"No. We slept in different rooms. I knew she wanted me to, but I couldn't. She threw herself at me, but I couldn't. As much as I felt that I needed a woman, I just couldn't do it. That night I met you, was the night I had decided to do it, but meeting you changed all that. After talking to you, I knew that you were the one for me. When I got back she was ready, but she turned mad when I told her that I had met the woman that is to be my wife. She was furious, but I did not let that get to me. I moved out and went to you."

"Are you telling me the truth?"

"Yes. I grieved my wife so much that I had no eyes for another woman, until you."

"I believe you, but why didn't you tell me this earlier?"

"You were keeping things from me and I wasn't really ready to face the decisions I really needed to make. I guess my flesh got in the way and I didn't trust God's Word like you did."

"William, I just wished you had told me?"

"When you mentioned her attentions, I refused to see it. In fact, I didn't want to see it. I felt that if I ignored it the children would stay longer. Honestly, I knew it and hoped you didn't' see it, but you can't keep anything from a child of God. I was so wrong, but a part of me didn't want to let go. I needed them to stay longer because of my own selfishness."

"Now that all this is out the way, where do we go from here?"

With no warning, I reached up and kissed my husband feverishly. I pulled away and smiled. Words could not fulfill what we thought No words were not needed. William knew like I did what was about to happen. From the couch to the floor, I made love for the first time to my husband, to the man God gave me.

The lovemaking took my breath away. I never thought that a man could make me feel that way, but my husband did. It was truly the one experience that my heart has taken a picture of. The way William made my body feel truly touched me. Never had my life been filled until then. I could not get enough of my husband. He called in to work for five days. All of those days were spent with me. William and I expressed our love like a man and a wife did. I did not get enough of him and likewise. That was the only time, I had not thought about God's Word because I was in the flesh. In the

flesh with my husband.

PHASE FOUR

Phase 4

William finally went back to work and I was alone and on what the world called a cloud nine. I was in love. I was really in love and it is not lust because many got the two mixed up. For a long time, I was the same way. What I felt as a child, I assumed that it was love, but it wasn't. With that in mind, I got up, bathed and prayed more earnestly than ever. It was like a whole new world had opened up to me. I decided to go see Sister Anna because the Lord placed her on my heart. Whenever God placed someone or something on your heart, you better obey and no matter how I felt about her, I still had to obey God.

I made my way to her place and I was nervous. I bounded the devil from using her against me and me against her. I took in a deep breath and knocked on the door. She didn't even ask who it was, Sister Anna opened the door and came out. I didn't expect her to let me in because the enemy knew who not to let in.

"What do you want?"

"I wanted to talk to you for a few, if it's ok?"

Sister Anna looked up at me and stated coolly, "Talk."

"I want you to know that I forgive you. I love you and most importantly, Christ loves you."

"I thought you had something to say."

"That was all."

I began to walk away. She spoke as to taunt me, "I thought you wanted to talk about how I had your dear Bishop first."

My blood wanted to boil, but I knew the voice of the evil one, when I hear it and I hear it. Turning around, I nicely walked back to her. I have on the armor of God and I am well protected. I wasn't led by God to come, but I wanted to come for my own personal reasons. I know she means well and I know she was held captive, but if she won't give up legal grounds there was nothing I could really do. I spoke with authority when I replied, "No. I don't receive accusations from God's arch enemy."

"It's me, Sister Anna. The deliverance worked."

I looked at her and I knew better. I knew that there were things she harbored in her heart and the devil himself would not let her or it go as quick. I knew that her deliverance was still at a standstill because it will take time to get her fully delivered and the few sessions we had was not nearly enough. With a smile, I spoke, "In the name of Jesus, I will speak as thus. Just because I have a nice house doesn't mean anything. Just because I am married to the man you love does not mean anything. Just because the Lord uses me to deliver people does not mean anything. The only thing that matters is what we do for God and what Jesus did for us at the cross. You don't get it, but your spiritual house is in a mess and needs rebuilding. Everything that isn't like Christ must be torn down, so Jesus can be the architect to build it on a sturdier foundation. Whenever you want wake up and realize that your deliverance is now at hand, tear up the devil's contract and hire Jesus."

Sister Anna spoke casually, "Very touchy, but this isn't about my deliverance. It's about your William, my Bishop. I've lowered my guard and allowed myself to be in a position I never dreamed of. I have found myself doing things out of my character. I didn't want these crept in unawares to address my life as such? How could I even imagine these feelings to explode as they have? I just don't understand why these emotions elevated as they did. But, you see, when my daughter and husband died, my love for God died. He is the reason why I am alone and bitter. He is the blame for all this."

"No he isn't. You can't and won't blame my God because of circumstances and situations that happened. He is in control of every aspect of your lives and if we don't want him to rule and rein in it than Satan will. I believe that is what has happen to you."

"I'm not the bad guy. I'm held hostage to my own heart and it won't let me go until I surrender to the notion that maybe just maybe he would love me. He needs love."

I cut her off to say, "The love you need only comes from Jesus because no other love will ever be good enough to sustain you."

"The sex is good isn't it."

I almost lost it, but I remembered the enemy knew how to get to you. I would not show any sign of fear. She will not know that she had gotten to me. Sadly enough, I saw that many demons have a strong hold on her. My spirit man could only grieve for the lost souls. I gave her a hug and walked off without looking back. I could only shake my feet as a testimony against her and keep going. My main purpose was to work on a foundation with my husband as learn from what we have been through and truly allow the love of God to overwhelm us and show us how to love as a husband and wife should.

Making home was wonderful. That day was the first time I looked at my home in a different light. I feel so at peace with my past that I can now expect a better future.

PHASE FIVE

PHASE FIVE

Weeks had gone by and we didn't see Sister Anna or the children. We were focusing on getting our marriage right that we relied on God when to visit the children. Things were wonderful and I never knew what real love from a man would feel like until I met my past head on and put it all behind me. I knew we say we let the Lord handle our demons, but do we really? Do we really let the Lord have it or do we take it back like we mostly do.

It was never easy to just let things go and let God do it, but we must. It is never to let the spiritual have it when we see it in our own eyes a way of handling it. Mainly it is because we can see actual results and don't have to wait on God to do as HE said HE would do in HIS Word. However, in many cases letting go is the best thing, but we won't see it until we really let it go and really let God have it.

I closed my thoughts as my husband and I arrived at the Jesus Saves Only Pentecostal Church. William opened the door. He held my hand and spoke, "You will do fine tonight. Allow Jesus to use you like I know HE will and does."

"I'm just nervous. It has been a few months since I spoke and everything. William it's so unlike me to be so emotional."

"It is understandable for you to be like this. I will be in the congregation and if you feel you can't do it, look at me."

"Ok."

My husband left me alone and went to the congregation. I prayed as I made my way to the podium. I did my usual scanning of the crowd. Taking a deep breath, I saw William and smiled. He gave me the earthly confidence I needed to go on.

"Many of you say you have faith in God, but do you know what it is to really have faith that God can and does deliver you? This evening, I will tell you my testimony. I don't mean how God has blessed me with a house, a car, or paid a bill or two. I don't mean how he blesses me with money or material things. I mean a real testimony of deliverance unto salvation. Many so call churches are like a cult and don't realize it. It is so easy to get caught up that it is scary; therefore, it is important for you to know who the Lord Jesus is to you, study your King James Version bible and live by HIS Spirit. You see, I was in a compound that had the Word of God all twisted up. They believed that sacrificing a child through the fire to Molech was the way for everyone in the group to go to Heaven, but it is not.

341

Their so called word was so saturated with lies that I an eight year old girl had a child that was sacrificed for what they called the New Era." The crowd gasps and began to pay full attention. To this crowd, a child having a child to be given up was unheard of but now they know. "I was tricked and to top it off, the baby was by my oldest brother. The Majesty Leader whom I never seen before until that day. I can talk about it now, but there was a time in my life that I could not mention what happened to me because I did not remember. I had placed my entire past in my past. I refused to think about what I had done because I didn't want to remember what I had done. But you see the enemy did not count on my mother to teach me the ways of Jesus Christ. He did not count on me surviving the night I saw my mother transformed into a beast straight out of Hell." The people said ooh in unison, but I continued,

342

"Hell is real and the devil, Satan, his emps and anything pertaining to him is real. You see that night at the church about thirty-four years ago, I was the only survivor in an attempt to deliver my mother. It is a scene I will not ever forget and the smell of burning flesh has not escaped my nose. Pastor's hands were cut off, hearts were taking out of chest, bodies were cut in halves, blood was everywhere, and black birds ate the people's flesh as I watched. You don't know what type of fatal end you could have when you proclaim the Word of God or you proclaim to be something the Lord did not call you to be. Please keep in mind the Lord will clean HIS house first."

The crowd was so quiet a pin could be heard if it fell. Clearing my throat, my voice was louder, "You see once Christ has delivered you, I mean truly redeemed you from the enemy and delivered you, you won't forget. No matter how you try, you can't forget it and by that the devil thought he ruined my life by the things I had gone through. He thought he had ruined me because I at the age of eight called myself in love with my brother. However, it wasn't until recently that I discovered my brother fact. Anyway, I suppressed those emotions, those memories. I was tricking myself into thinking that, if I forget, it will go away. If I don't remember then it didn't happen, but you see, I could not go forward until I fixed my past. I could not really be happy until I faced what was holding me in the jail of self-condemnation. An average girl would have been ruined because of those injustices. An average girl would have given up and doubted God and lost what faith she had, but I am here to tell you, in order to believe God can you must have faith that God will do the things you need done. My entire life has been built

344

on Jesus Christ. Even through the hardest times in my life, Christ still delivered me. When I felt alone and discouraged, HE still delivered me. I didn't think I could make it, but here I stand today, sealed, and delivered by Jesus Christ." Everywhere I walked the people's eyes followed. Every gesture of my hands or head, was watched by the people. I said, "Tonight I will give you a story. It is a story for the human heart. Many of you in here, cannot eat meat, some of you that are eating meat can't swallow sound doctrine because you have been exposed to the wrong kind of meat. Please bow your heads as I pray." I saw my husband's face and once again he gave me that encouraging smile. Like the rest of the people, I bowed my head and spoke, "Lamb of God, for this reason you have me to tell them a story. One I believe is ordained by you to do. Close their natural ears on what they hear and open the spiritual

ears of their heart.

Your Word says: one waters it, one plants it, but

it's YOU that gives the increase. Tonight, as I plant the

seed, allow their faith to water it as YOU increase it. In

your name Jesus, I pray Amen, Amen. The name Karen

is a Greek name that means Pure, Clear and Beloved of

God. All week Karen had been watching the signs in

the sky the way her grandfather taught her many years

ago; however, this was one thing she was glad she

remembered from her people's ways. She stood on her

family's porch because there was uneasiness about, the

day. Turning her eyes toward the sky the things she

noticed made her look more earnestly. The trees were

telling a story in the wind as it shook her and

everything around her. In that instant the sun decided to

take cover, while the clouds began to run in the sky and

from a distance she could smell the rain, but see the hail coming straight towards her. Right then she knew, the storm had made it. Quick in her thinking she took off behind the house to the cellar but unable to move fast because the wind was pushing her backwards. Beating against her body vigorously was the hail as it broke the windows out of her house and left bruises on her body. Her entire thought was, "if I don't make it, I'll be lost." Karen without thinking thought about how the Children of Israel and how they were trapped at the Red Sea, she thought about how the people went in circles for forty years lost and she thought about how if people do not come to Christ they will be lost. So, being determined not to be as those were she continued to press her way. Struggling to open the heavy doors she used the faith of her Lord to make it inside. Looking around she placed a medium stick through the door loops to help hold them

347

together. Pulling her straight auburn hair from her face, she looked pass the food and water for a seat. While sitting her senses became keen to the environment, such as, things being thrown around by an angry wind, the crackling of thunder and by the door hinge Yes flashes of lightening feeling more afraid, Karen turned around, got on her knees and began to pray.

Once on her knees and deeply involved in conversation with her Savior she heard not when the storm stopped. Smiling because she weathered the storm she cared how not her house looked because she was alive and well. Karen tried to push open the doors, but couldn't something was holding her in. She tried everything she could think of. She went from hitting the doors repeatedly and screaming for help, to taking the hinges down, but thought the weight of whatever it was would fall on her. For hours she sat in the chair and thought about what to do. *I could make a firm grip with my feet and take my shoulder to push against the door* she thought. When that idea would prove to be a bust she would sit again to think. For hours more she sat there and sat there, thinking about what to do. Finally the idea hit her she would take the small stick like a bat and try to beat loudly against it, she thought, but that didn't work, either. She was getting worried and scared so she opened some food and ate. Feeling tired, she rested on the small mat she had prepared for a time as such and slept. She woke up and assumed she heard someone outside so she started hollering and screaming, but no one was there. Again, she started back using her feet and shoulders to budge the door, but it was still too heavy. Karen was tired, but did not give up. At one point she would bump the doors where they met and they would only come back down on her. Sitting on the top step she tried to use her back to move the doors, but that did not help; therefore, she lay back down and slept. Over the next five days she would remain calm, and then act like a wild woman pulling at the doors. In between trying to get out and eating she would sleep. On day seven the grief of never being found over took her and she began to cry as she hit the door as if it had done something to her and saying *let me out, let me out,* but nothing happened. Karen sat up now because she was getting worried and the thought of never being found alive cave in, with sadness she lay up and cried more.

Suddenly in the middle of night she woke up and now more clearer she realize that being trapped was not the problem, having something over the doors was not the problem, looking for everything to help her was not the problem and sitting around thinking on what she could do was not the problem. As if a light went on in her mind, immediately she knew that not praying and believing in her Lord was the problem. "How could I be so naïve and forget that he knows everything and sees all? How could I forget that he knows I am here and sometimes he places us where we don't want to be just to have us to depend on him? How could I forget that His word says that HE will never leave me nor forsake me? Feeling like a fool Karen in haste got on her knees and prayed like never before. When she got up she felt relieved, but she was still trapped. She didn't feel led to touch the doors so she sat in the chair and rejoiced to the knowledge that no matter where she was at her God sees her and no matter what it looked like he still see her. While being trapped in the cellar she came to the conclusion that her Jesus wanted her to focus on HIM and not her situation and that was why she was trapped with no way out but through HIM."

Before stepping down I scanned the crowd again and saw that many were speechless. With a final word, I commanded them, "I dare you to find Christ before it is too late. Some People will not ever come to the knowledge that HE is the I AM, that I AM. Don't let it be too late because like others that have died without HIM, they don't have the chance you have. Pray for me as I pray for you in the Lord."

EPILOGUE

Grace had her only child. She names her Hannah Faith Dalton. Sister Anna went mad and had to be placed in a mental facility because she became a danger to herself as well as the twins. The children reside with William and Grace. They have Jesus as their foundation.

www.ingramcontent.com/pod-product-compliance
Lightning Source LLC
Chambersburg PA
CBHW031427240626
47154CB00001B/233